ECOQUEEN

THE SUPERHERO WITH THE POWER TO REVERSE CLIMATE CHANGE

JOANNA MEASER KANOW

SEAS OF TREES

Published by Seas of Trees Publishing, Telluride, Colorado

Edited and designed by Girl Friday Productions
www.girlfridayproductions.com

Design: Paul Barrett
Project management: Alexander Rigby and Laura Dailey

ISBN (paperback): 978-1-7365987-0-2
ISBN (ebook): 978-1-7365987-1-9

This book is dedicated to my daughters, Ayla and ShaiAnn, who are part of the next generation who can help repair the balance on earth. And to my mom, Merle Measer, who showed me how to sit down and write a story that must be told.

We are the first generation to feel the impact of climate change and the last generation that can do something about it.

—US president Barack Obama in his remarks at the UN Climate Change Summit, September 23, 2014, quoting Seattle mayor Mike McGinn's open letter to the president of Harvard University

Sometimes we just simply have to find a way. The moment we decide to fulfill something, we can do anything. And I'm sure that the moment we start behaving as if we were in an emergency, we can avoid climate and ecological catastrophe. Humans are very adaptable: we can still fix this. But the opportunity to do so will not last for long. We must start today. We have no more excuses.

—Greta Thunberg speaking to UK Parliament, April 23, 2019

CHAPTER 1

LET IT RIP

RURAL RUSSIA, PRESENT DAY

Was it wrong to destroy something that was causing harm to all living things? EcoQueen wished her latest mission did not have to be undoing her own father's work, but she also knew that mining and burning this one part of the earth was creating more of a problem than it was solving. The world knew that the burning of fossil fuels was largely contributing to the global warming crisis, but nobody seemed to be doing anything to try to change this global addiction. So, EcoQueen decided it was a legitimate time for her to use her superpowers and stand up against climate change.

Here she was, throwing a monkey wrench into the world's newest, largest coal-fired plant, one that would burn as much fossil fuel into the atmosphere a day as Switzerland burned in a year. She wondered why they called this place a *plant* when it was the opposite of nature sprouting and blooming into something beautiful. It was the antithesis of a plant. It was a destruction of nature and had already done so much damage to soil, air, and water—even before it was fully operational. Therefore, by destroying it, EcoQueen would be standing up for all living things that would be affected by the pollution.

Something in her aligned with the concept that all life was sacred, like indigenous groups knew, that the earth should be revered, and defending it took precedence over profits. EcoQueen needed to intervene and disrupt the pattern. It's a crime to kill a human, but what EcoQueen couldn't understand was how it could be acceptable to kill whole ecosystems, habitats, and species as part of an economic plan.

It was clear that her role was to assure that no further significant harm would occur. If the adults were not standing up for the future of her generation, EcoQueen had to use her superpowers to do something about it. Time was running out. Those who created the problem of climate change would die of old age, and her generation would die from climate change. Unless she acted now.

Eight security guards were stationed on the power plant's perimeter. Their job was to secure the facility, allowing only those important people and top financiers who were invited to the opening ceremony ribbon cutting scheduled for later that day. The business of power had earned some enemies, but the coal burners had plenty of money to burn on a celebration of what would be the trophy of the biggest coal power plant on earth. Power plant money was as dirty as its technology.

Today was a big achievement for her dad, who programmed the software that the new power plant was utilizing, but not so much for the rest of the planet. EcoQueen knew that the world did not need additional carbon released into the environment, but somehow the power plant sold itself as new green technology. The plant's smokestacks stood by, ready to release noxious gases like carbon dioxide as a byproduct of the coal-fired steam turbines. A dangerous mix of new chemical vapors was about to be introduced to the region in sickening quantities. The smokestacks were the dominant feature on the horizon of this Russian landscape now, in this small, little-known rural town in middle Russia. The stacks against the skyline looked like oversize cigarettes lined up, pillars of unartistic concrete monoliths.

EcoQueen surprised herself with unexpected poise when she came splashing out of the LCD screen of the computer monitor, one of many that sat atop a cold concrete surface in the control room of the power plant. Boots first, she flew out of the screen with her feet and spandex-covered legs leading the way, followed by her small torso—topped with a cape tied on the shelf of her clavicles—and finally, her tousled black hair, which whipped forward. Once she was out of the screen, she tossed her hair back from her face. She nailed the graceful dismount with a tuck-and-roll move. EcoQueen was almost tempted to add an official gymnast's salute to her best exit yet. After the wild ride, during which she had held on for dear life to the fiber-optic cable teletransporting her through broadband internet, she was glad to stop moving at such high speed. EcoQueen took a moment to catch her breath while she got properly situated for the mission at hand. She felt slightly disoriented from the unusual mode of travel but was eager to get started.

Río had prepped her well. Her twin brother, whom she had yet to meet in person—because they were separated in infancy—had been organizing from mission control in another hemisphere, and together they had attended to all the important details. EcoQueen knew what to expect. That didn't mean that there wasn't some room for improvisation, though. She carefully assessed the scene in the main control room. The new coal-fired plant that was poised to break all the records in power production, as well as destructive environmental impact, and the hardware behind it were impressive.

The soles on EcoQueen's knee-high black faux leather boots did not make a squeak on the sterile tiled floor. Her hooded cape fluttered gently at her calves as she stealthily approached the megacomputers that would be fired up for the launch. She pulled the hood up so she could have the best audio from Río at HQ. EcoQueen's tight suit defined her petite yet strong body. Her small-framed hips, powerful glutes, and compact sides drew attention to her obliques, which looked like they were grabbing her body and holding her up. Her muscles sat on top of her featherweight bones like frosting. Back at school and home, in her non-superhero life as the blend-into-the-woodwork high school student Kora, she preferred comfort over style and mostly wore loose-fitting pants with a hoodie sweatshirt. But on missions, she was thankful for her high-tech superhero suit because its temperature-regulating nanotech material adapted to whichever climate crisis she was addressing. The sensors in the suit automatically adjusted so her body temperature would stay comfortable even in a slightly cooled room like the one she was standing in. Her superhero outfit was fitted for performance and not for sex appeal, so it never made her self-conscious, just powerful.

Inside the room with the most cutting-edge instruments and technologies in the field, EcoQueen took great care not to touch anything with her lethal electrical charge—not just yet. She could taste the air filtration system that was already battling the everyday dust and condensation that could slowly destroy computers. As she positioned herself for action, she thought of children on the other side of the world who would possibly be spared from another inch of sea level rising, or those who would not have to live through another typhoon, hurricane, or drought, if she only could do something bold now.

EcoQueen knew what she needed to do. Even if it might appear like a malevolent act of vandalism, how could it be wrong to stand up against something that could cause such harm? Property and investments were at stake, but in her mind, there were also kids' futures, the environment, and the health of people near and far to consider. Was it acceptable to try and stop something that could do so much damage? She had already made that ethical decision.

She was excited to use her electrical powers. She spent so much time and energy in her life as Kora trying to control, hide, and suppress them. But now, as EcoQueen, she felt good about letting them rip, finally. She knew she possessed superpowers, and she knew she was meant to use them to accomplish good changes. She had just been waiting to know it was time to unleash them. She had been spending her life trying to keep them contained, but her heart and her hands were certain that the time had come to let go.

The mission took mere seconds. EcoQueen raised her hands up and down in front of her as if shaking out a sheet in slow motion, building the energy. Her delicate hands did not appear to be weapons, but they were about to be. She only stood at a fierce five feet two (five feet three in her motorcycle boots with the heels that had the computer chips, springs, and grounding rods installed in them). Despite her XS sizing, she was a force of nature. Her eyes closed in a type of meditation. Because of the high voltage that extended out from her fingertips, all she needed to do was touch the machines plugged into the power plant's network to get the job done.

Like a lightning strike, hotter than fire, the spark she sent out blasted the entire electrical system of the building. High-voltage current flowed through the circuitry on the interior and exterior of the plant. The control room and all the systems beyond were completely fried by the immense power surge, not much different from what happens to a microwave when you put foil in it.

Screens shattered, needles in the gauges flapped back and forth from zero to red, and the wiring crackled. The machines and all their microchips, motherboards, operating systems, memory, and processors sparked, melted, flatlined, and died an electrocuted death. The smell of burnt plastic combined with something like burnt popcorn filled the room.

It was what EcoQueen and Río had planned, but it still brought wonder that the simple touch of her fingers to the computer could cause such systemic damage. It was almost too easy, she thought. The short circuit and internal havoc her touch created were like an invisible terminal disease, like a stroke or heart attack that overwhelmed the power plant's system and killed it, and that gave EcoQueen a hit of satisfaction. Triumphantly, she sang, "Another one bites the dust." And she was already thinking about what her next mission to protect the earth might be.

EcoQueen waited for Río to initiate her recall through the fried fiber-optic cables. She knew Río had his hands at the ready on the teletransport controls and was dead focused on facilitating her swift exit through the algorithm he'd built. But as the seconds ticked by, EcoQueen started getting nervous. She called through her microphone, "Get me out of here, Río! Get me back, bro, they're coming!"

After a few tense moments of silence, she heard Río again. "I know, I know. I'm working on it, EcoQueen." Though she normally traveled through fiber-optic cables, Río had recently tweaked the teletransport algorithm so it would link with her powers and take her anywhere via cable, Wi-Fi, or satellite. She knew it could adapt to almost any communication technology, but EcoQueen was starting to worry. She couldn't afford glitches!

Trying to control her breathing and not panic, EcoQueen noticed some guards around the corner while emergency alarms began to sound, emitting alerts for the failure of the system. She crouched under a cold metal desk and whispered, "Río, it's time for me to go!"

Finally, he came back on the line, relief in his voice. "Use that computer on the far left."

EcoQueen placed her hand on the screen. As quickly as she had entered the scene, she was gone. She went flying through the computer back to her dad's iPad in California. Her dad was probably just learning of the major malfunction at the coal-fired plant and would soon be tasked with a yearlong project of getting it up and running again.

Instantaneously back in her street clothes, Kora rested for a minute. On the counter, her legs hung off the edge, not long enough to touch the ground, and Kora thought about what she had just done.

CHAPTER 2

THE SACRED SEED

THE AMAZONIAN RAINFOREST, EIGHTEEN YEARS EARLIER

In a remote patch of the Amazonian rainforest in Ecuador, on land where the Waorani indigenous tribe had lived for centuries without much contact with the modern world, Joaquin, a twenty-seven-year-old local, quietly climbed the chain-link fence. He tried not to rattle it when he swung his legs over and landed on a span of dirt that no longer belonged to him or his people.

The Waorani, who numbered around two thousand, once maintained one of the largest territories of all Amazonian indigenous people in Ecuador. Their land was being encroached on now because it appeared to be sitting on a jackpot of oil. The national government had written into the constitution—overnight, it seemed—that it had the right to develop land to extract oil and gas, regardless of who it belonged to.

Joaquin had never seen a chain-link fence before the Vena Principal Compañía moved in seven months ago, claiming the dirt as theirs to unearth.

He had no experience dealing with boundary lines quite like this, made from metal posts and curls of barbed wire strung to keep people who lived there out. Joaquin always thought that his land was protected since it was entrusted to his people as shepherds of the earth. But now it was being gutted—surgery without permission. The forest was being

attacked by humans who felt there was more to it than just the standing trees and the rich ecosystem they supported. The Compañía was
after what was beneath the ground, the crude oil.

But the Waorani knew that their land had the greatest value when
it was treated with respect instead of plundered. Joaquin lived in one of
the last pristine Amazonian rainforests on the planet, and he and his
tribe were the only ones who were willing and able to protect it.

It was a typical sticky warm night in the rainforest, and the slight
breeze cooled him just enough to keep the sweat on his forehead from
dripping down into his eyes. The hum of diesel motors, the squeak of
unoiled backhoe gears, and the backing-up beeps of heavy machinery
had paused for the night. Regardless, the jungle bugs still made their
sounds in concert. A natural symphony turned up the volume of the
night.

The nighttime jungle was never quiet. The chatter of nocturnal
canopy birds and crickets mixed with the pings and chirps of tree frogs
in stereo. The Waorani villagers who lived there found comfort in these
sounds. The hubbub told them that their ancestral home was healthy,
that it still teemed with life, that the relentless march of oil wells and
logging into the jungle hadn't reached them quite yet. But it was close.

A healthy jungle still existed on each side of the space that had been
mowed down for oil exploration. Joaquin's way of life had been largely
unchanged from that of his ancestors centuries ago. But increasingly,
he saw oil spills contaminate the jungle and eliminate the game his
indigenous people depended on. Cocoa and coffee plantations were
encroaching on the rainforest as well. He knew precisely the stakes
for which he fought. *We do not want to disappear. We must keep our
homeland in a delicate balance.* But the first of ninety-seven oil wells
planned to sprout was already creating unprecedented devastation to
the land.

The Compañía gambled that they would find a fountain underground that would erupt in thick black crude so people in distant
countries and cities could happily use it for their cars, houses, and air-
plane flights. Joaquin and his people knew that this ancient substance
was meant to stay safely tucked in the earth and that only problems
would arise if it were disturbed.

Dreams mattered. When Joaquin was a toddler, the elders began having intense visions about an imminent threat coming from the external world. And then they started to witness the destruction and the demise of natural habitats. After generations as stewards of the land, they learned that the western edge of their homeland was being claimed and ravaged by the Compañía. Foreigners who were strangers to the Amazon forest and its way of life ransacked their home. The oil company was hungry to strike it rich on the estimated 4.7 billion barrels of crude resting underground.

The tribe's prophecy, the one that predicted a massive attack on Mother Earth that would tear open the face of the earth to a point of irreparable destruction, seemed to be playing itself out right in front of Joaquin's eyes. Trees lay slashed, downed, and dragged to clear room for further exploitation. If trees could scream, it would sound like a murder scene. Gone was the habitat, the home, of every living thing that depended on the trees for food, for shade, for shelter, for security.

Joaquin couldn't believe it was happening, but he knew he was responsible for doing something about it.

Joaquin tried to calm his nerves and his racing heartbeat by feeling all parts of his flat, tough feet touch the ground. The earth upon which he stood felt dead and foreign to him. The jungle that was once so dense, with its hot, moist canopy, had created an ecosystem of its own from the foliage that shaded the busy world of the forest. Where he stood now had been reduced to a buzz cut, like a closely shaven bald head, the type that represents hatred and violence.

Although Joaquin had not yet journeyed much farther than the boundaries of his rainforest and admittedly had a limited understanding of the wider world, he knew it was not right to harm their Mother Earth, their higher-power deity, which they called Aweidi. Joaquin was of the generation bridging tradition and technology, a generation that was becoming less isolated due to increasing access. His parents still committed to dressing traditionally, while Joaquin and his friends wore more Western clothes. The elders still lived in huts called *malookas* woven out of palm fronds, yet Joaquin's hut and the science center he built for ecotourists were constructed with concrete blocks. And while they hunted using blowguns and poison darts to get their fish and meat for the day, the Wi-Fi kicked on every night so Joaquin was able to learn about life beyond his sacred land.

With a little bit of cellular access, Joaquin was exposed to that which was not right in front of him. He was one of the first in his tribe to own a smartphone. The science center that brought in foreigners to learn about his jungle and culture introduced him to current events as well as history and other cultures.

A year ago, a visiting Dutch scientist had shown Joaquin a map with a green circle drawn around the Waorani territory, which was officially part of the ten-thousand-square-kilometer Parque Nacional Yasuní. For the first time, Joaquin also saw a red line that marked the *Bloque de petróleo*—areas where the Ecuadorian government had allowed oil exploration and drilling, despite the national park being a UNESCO Biosphere Reserve. And that is when he learned that their land was under attack.

A bulldog bat flew over Joaquin's head and tripped the motion-sensor security lights, which triggered the drone security video cameras to look for movement.

Floodlights electrified the area as bright as the sun at high noon, suddenly illuminating the oil field. Hopefully, Joaquin had not been caught on camera. The Compañía had already been tracking Joaquin and was waiting for a misstep so they could remove him from the scene as they had done to his uncle, Sol, who went missing eight months ago.

Knowing that he had only minutes to spare before the alarms began to sound, Joaquin sprinted to the edge of the drilling operation and looked down the hole that had been dug almost fifteen thousand feet into the core of the earth to hit the oil hidden so deep. He inched his toes up to the edge.

He removed the satchel from around his neck and opened it. Two dark red, parched, teardrop-shaped seeds rested in the suede pouch. His people before him had safely guarded these exact seeds for hundreds of years. Joaquin had been chosen to protect the seeds for the last decade, and like the keepers of the seed for the generations before him, he prayed every day that he would never be the one called upon to use them. But it was evident that now was the time.

Joaquin massaged the sacred seeds, one in each hand. The circumstances made him feel sure in his bones that it was time to sow a sacred seed. He returned one safely to the leather satchel around his neck just in case things got even worse and he had to use it in the future. He rolled the other seed gently between his fingertips, feeling the potential energy, the magic in it about to burst.

The seeds were the last hope for his tribe, his people—all people. If he somehow faltered or failed to use this seed for its intended purpose, Joaquin felt that he would be the only one to blame for failing to preserve his ancestral lands—and he would be responsible for the end of the world as he knew it. The future of the forest that his grandparents and parents had preserved for him was in peril, but the sacred seed would save it for his children and grandchildren. There was no other way.

He heard the ceremonial chanting of the war cry of his tribe's people, and he could not tell if the sound was real or imagined. The time had come to stand up and protect the Amazon forest from further destruction in the name of progress and profit. With a kiss to his fingers, an offering to the sky gods, and a tap on the earth, Joaquin fulfilled his sober role as the last in the line of the keepers of the seeds and tossed one of the seeds down the pipeline. He was more agile with his poisoned spear than a tossed seed, but it was enough. The sacred seed free-fell almost three miles down . . . down . . . down the man-made gaping hole that was created for the oil drill, but which also made a great hole for planting a seed.

He was sweating from his temples, and the back of his T-shirt was soaked with perspiration, not just from the jungle heat, but from sheer adrenaline and fear of what was about to happen. His hand trembled, his jaw clenched, and his eyes did not blink as he waited to witness the magnitude of his actions. Joaquin knew the seeds held powers, but he had been unsure of their extent. All kinds of lore had been passed down about the potential of the planted seed, but nobody knew for sure what would happen. Or, what if the seeds were duds? What if they were too old and they no longer held the magic of rapid regrowth and overnight accelerated reforestation that the elders had spoken of? Joaquin only knew that he was responsible for planting seeds when it looked like the end of the world was near.

He remembered the ceremony when he was seventeen years old. The shaman had looked gravely into his eyes and whispered, "We select you, Joaquin, as the next keeper of the seeds. Do what you know to be right. The fight for Mother Earth is the mother of all fights."

From the long line of trusted hands that had held the sacred seeds for generations, gravity lovingly took over and guided the seed to where it needed to land, deep in the earth. The perfect combination of soil, water, and sunlight would bring out the perfectly stored full potential of the magical seed, but it was already launching into stimulated growth and essential life-saving, life-sustaining forest restoration. Once Joaquin released one half of his precious, sacred inheritance from his grip and his care, he was well aware that everything had changed.

Upon touchdown, the seed sprouted. As Joaquin pivoted for his fast exit after the seed was dropped, germination had already begun. The roots started forming and the stems started pushing up through the ground—the seed had split open and started to propagate and morph into the separate eighty thousand plant species that make up a healthy Amazon rainforest. Nature never rushes, but in these times of distress, this was the point of the magical seeds; vegetation grew at hyperspeed, in desperation and glory. On some kind of magical fast-forward, the seed grew to maturity, not just as one species, but as an entire integrated, lush, healthy, biodiverse rainforest five miles square. It filled what had just that night been void and cowed land back to its original density. Leaves unfurled, roots splayed down. Overlapping vines, flowers, fruits, branches, and trunks intertwined, wrapping around each other as if holding hands. Entangled in the branches were hints of some yellow-painted metal, now that trucks hung in trees as if they were cheap plastic Christmas ornaments. It was like a time-lapse but in real life, from seed to sapling to a grown tree in a matter of hours. Overnight reforestation.

The rate of growth was impressive, but still not as fast as forests were cut: every 1.2 seconds humans destroy an area of forest the size of a football field. The sacred seed was the only way to level the playing field—warp speed the regeneration almost as fast as the forests were being cut down. It usually takes decades for a forest to become mature, and seconds to chainsaw it down.

One never gets to observe grass growing, or flowers at the moment they unfurl to bloom, but growth to maturity happened almost instantly in the rainforest. There was no time to wait. The earth needed the Amazon forest to be healthy and thriving.

A feeling of relief melted down Joaquin's tensed, adrenaline-filled body, followed by a quick feeling of accomplishment before the fight-or-flight instinct set in. And he knew he had to run for it.

This was the moment the shaman had prepared him for. Joaquin could smell the burning wood of cooking fires in his village, the same kind of wood from which they built their furniture. He wanted to return to his hut and cuddle in bed with his girlfriend, Avalon, a visiting scientist from Australia. There was no time for such comfort. By the time Joaquin got to the barrier fences he had jumped to get in, sprouts had covered the deserted land, unfurling like fiddleheads, spirals unraveling, and blanketing like frilled turf. Joaquin had no choice but to run from the company's fences, under the floodlights, on video surveillance. "Trespassing," "vandalizing," "terrorizing," they would call what he'd done, but he was just protecting the land that was the health of the world.

The forest itself seemed to grow to protect him from the drones' line of sight, but he could not risk being captured. He ran in a full sprint right past his hut, his village, his familiar jungle, the only home he had ever known. He had to keep running, past his parents' garden where they grew the best berries, past his grandparents' hut where he had just helped them replace their thatched roof, past the suspension bridge where he kissed Avalon for the first time. He sprinted past the mangroves where the shaman had given him this responsibility as keeper of the seeds. His arms pumped, and his feet knew the paths to take as he passed his favorite spring where every drop of water he ever drank came from, the cave where he feared the puma lived when he was a kid, the tree house he built with his best friend, Jossa, near the secret rock.

He ran because he could not go back. Even though his people would celebrate him as a hero, the Vena Principal Compañía would consider him a criminal for disrupting their business and their profits. Joaquin had fought destruction with regrowth. He undid a multimillion-dollar business enterprise by planting one special seed. In just hours, from what he understood now about the seed, the cleared land would be completely overgrown.

Where the Compañía had denuded the earth, now the earth healed. Every step that hit the soil as he ran landed on a soft patch of the new growth. The magic of the seed had orchestrated life to begin, and within hours, life would be in full bloom in a new forest.

As Joaquin hurried to escape, all the arid dusty ground filled in, blanketed with sprouts, delicate stems, and brand-new baby leaves. And then evidence of flowers, and then fruits fell to the ground, only to sprout more trees almost instantaneously. From these roots a full forest canopy touched the sky. As if Mother Nature was in cahoots with the magic, a spontaneous and fortuitous heavy rainfall introduced the perfect moisture that layered on the leaves of every tree like a sponge bath. Beads of water clung to plant life, textured and vital, as they reached for the sun that was just starting to rise. Life began with water—singing, quenching, sparking life.

The roots mingled belowground to create a new ecosystem there, and more life arose. These rapid magical new-birth forests shared an interconnected root system that was thick and entangled, as strong as stainless steel, elaborate and efficient as a braided freeway system beneath the soil. Gnarled and healthy branches spread and locked arms like a nonviolent protest. With the overnight brand-new jungle growth, the wind could be heard again, rustling in the waxy foliage. The damp fragrance of the forest returned.

The accelerated reforestation had upturned the vehicles on-site, severed pipes, collapsed excavation sites, toppled oil rigs, and wholly and successfully disrupted the entire drilling operation. Only minimal evidence of the company's work was left. The jungle absorbed what was human made and turned it back into the dirt. The new growth overtook anything that was not meant to be there. Like a flower growing up from a crack in the sidewalk, this forest had fought to come back. The wounds that humanity inflicted were undone overnight.

***

When the men in hard hats reported back for their shifts the next morning, they could not find their worksite. The trailer where they drank their coffee from Styrofoam cups was not where they remembered. The fences delineating the "off-limits" areas had vaporized.

The denuded oil field they had spent weeks clearing was no longer a barren space but rather filled in as densely as the forest from outside the boundary. There was no way to explain it beyond witchcraft. The workers were not the type to believe in superstition, yet they were a bit spooked. Among themselves, they quietly wondered if some kind of curse had been set on them for tampering with the natural balance.

Private investigators, police, and even some military personnel joined the hunt for the vandal who did this.

The police pursued Joaquin for what they were calling an act of terrorism, or at least vandalism, because of the destruction of the machines, land movers, and tools that had been used for the drilling operation. Different military-outfitted law enforcement, hired by the Compañía, barged into the hut where Avalon had been living with Joaquin for the last several months.

Avalon had not planned to stay in the Amazon. She had not planned on falling in love there. But sometimes love is like that. The rainforest, the community, and even the hut Avalon had made home had felt comforting with Joaquin as her partner, but now that he had disappeared, she felt more foreign than someone trying to use a euro to buy a pack of Tim Tams back in Sydney.

Now, for the third time in the week since Joaquin planted the sacred seed and left his village on foot, an armed group of five men interrogated Avalon, rifling through her belongings, asking where Joaquin was.

"I'm telling you for the hundredth time, I don't know where he is. I went to sleep with him in this bed, and when I woke in the morning, he was gone. I have no idea how he disappeared. I'm scared about what could have happened to him, and you don't seem to have any sympathy or understanding!"

They knew that she was Australian and could have her embassy on them if they misstepped. But big money had been lost, so they would find the vandal responsible. Joaquin was known as an intellectual, a leader, an organizer, a shaman, and a warrior against the Compañía in a war that indigenous people had mostly lost. He was now being treated like a criminal . . . if they could find him.

Just minutes after Avalon's inquisitors stomped out of the hut, Joaquin's mother, Rosa, knocked. Avalon welcomed her in. Rosa carried a jug of her famous chicha drink. She poured the saliva-fermented liquid into a dinged-up stainless steel bowl and offered it to Avalon.

Avalon had tried this homemade jungle booze before with Joaquin. She knew that it was made from many mouths that chewed up and spit out boiled yucca plants, but also knew that it packed a punch, so she happily shared the bowl with Rosa. She elected not to think about the science of the spit enzyme that converted the starch into a simple sugar to cause the fermentation. What she thought of instead while she sipped on the watery, milkshake-like beverage was that it could help take the edge off her fear and grief.

"*Mija*, do not worry about my son. He will be OK. I trust that Joaquin is just in hiding. He is smart and swift." Rosa gently reassured his son's girlfriend, but she secretly wished someone would give her the same kind of pep talk. "He probably would not have told you, but he has had much training to survive. Ever since he was entrusted with our tribe's sacred seeds, we have known that he might be called to act, and that might mean he would have to evade the authorities."

Avalon's ears perked up. "What is a sacred seed? Is that how the forest grew back overnight?"

"You will have to talk to the shaman about this, I cannot tell you all, but it is a seed that our ancestors have passed down for seven generations. Joaquin was right to do what he did. This was the moment to plant it." Rosa gave Avalon a sad smile, wanting to show her as much love as she could without revealing all their secrets.

Avalon could not stop thinking about Joaquin's last words to her: "I have to plant some seeds." He had kissed her in bed and left through their wooden front door with the overly springy hinge that made it swing shut with authority.

When he left, she had no idea that she was never going to see him again.

A month after he'd gone, Avalon was still in Joaquin's village. She had planned to come to the rainforest for a short time and gather a few extra data points on forest restoration for the research she was working on in Beijing. Her plan was to learn enough to put the finishing touches on her stadium-size indoor rainforest project back in China that would scrub the atmosphere clean, not to fall in love and live with a man who would disappear, and then wait for him indefinitely. It had been six months since she left Beijing, and she didn't know when she would return to her mini-ecosystem atmospheric mitigation project, which was already under construction.

She lay awake watching the bugs congregate on the special double bug-net system Joaquin built around the bedposts of their sleeping spot to make sure the mosquito-bite-prone Avalon could feel secure in a bug-proof womb. The supersized mosquitoes, grasshoppers, and other antennaed, unidentifiable bloodthirsty insects patiently waited on the other side of the netting, smelling her sweet blood.

Without Joaquin, she thought, *Why am I still here?*

CHAPTER 3

KORA'S NOT LIKE OTHER KIDS

CALIFORNIA

At age two, Kora's first word was "Why?"

At age three, she refused to wear shoes and keep her clothes on.

At age four, she talked to imaginary friends and played in their imaginary world.

At age five, she refused to brush her hair, and it almost became dreadlocked, which is when her mother, Blythe, gave her a short pixie cut.

At age six, Kora's best friend was her dog, Zuma, and she didn't need anything else for entertainment besides him, paper, and colored pencils.

At age seven, all she wanted to do was read all day. When she was not reading, she was riding her bike on the bluff trail, singing songs that she made up to herself.

At age eight, she declared she was a vegetarian because she did not want to harm any animals.

At age nine, she was still tiny for her age.

At age twelve, the first fire broke out in her house.

It wasn't exactly your typical childhood.

Before Kora came along, Blythe Greenway had worked endless hours to gain status at her law firm that catered to high-value start-ups and venture capitalists. Then she woke up one day, alarmed—as if she had left the house without her cell phone—panicked, and scrambling because, somewhere along the way, she forgot to have a baby. After a good half decade of trying naturally and artificially to make a baby happen, she decided to try one last time and decided on adoption to get her baby.

When it came to paperwork, she dominated. Blythe could get through spreadsheets, PowerPoints, and applications like a boss because she was one.

Her husband, Duncan, didn't seem to be in as much of a rush. He could never fully envision being a parent as clearly as Blythe did. So all the roadblocks and delays that had come up in Blythe's having-a-baby mission didn't bother him.

Exactly eighteen months after the home visit and interviews, Blythe received a phone call from their social worker at the adoption agency. All her hard work had paid off, and she and Duncan were given the green light to bring home their baby girl. They had arrived at the finish line, where it was all going to begin.

After a grueling and emotional journey to Quito, Ecuador, on March 4, 2003, they finally brought their daughter home to live with them. Overnight, they became parents, and she was their daughter. They named their baby Kora Ariel Greenway. She had a different name when she was in the orphanage in Quito, but they wanted to give her their own name and start fresh. Not much was known about her first year in Ecuador, so they started right from the moment she made them a real, complete family, and they never looked back.

Kora was a silent baby, taking it all in—the new parents, new country, new smells, voices, people, food, colors, textures. Her hair was dark, thick, and straight like a horse's mane, but not yet long enough to tame in a neat ponytail. Her eyes were an emerald green that seemed electric alongside her dark brown sepia skin tone. She was on the smaller side.

Little Kora had an old soul, as if she knew something everyone else did not. It came out in how she looked around and observed, very tuned in to her surroundings. She focused so intently. Kora bathed in the new feeling of love and belonging.

Blythe and Kora were both shocked by how profoundly they could dive into loving so intensely. Kora had been starved for love and touch, and Blythe already felt that this baby was her most excellent teacher in life. Becoming a mom propelled Blythe into a new existence and purpose. It amazed Blythe how effortlessly she shook off her old way of making her work her life, to make her family her main priority. She took her ultra productivity and laser focus for accomplishment from the corporate world and redirected it into family life. She did not want to miss a single moment of this experience of raising her one and only child.

Kora's father, Duncan, on the other hand, took a little longer to warm up to being a dad. He was the kind of man who saw having a child as a reason to work even harder at the office. He knew his strengths lay in doing business and coding software rather than getting down on the floor on a blanket to play a slobbery game with a baby that couldn't even talk yet. He was looking forward to when the kid could do something with him, like shooting hoops or helping brew beer with his home garage kit. Until then, he embedded himself even deeper into work at his software start-up company.

The Greenway family home was on a much-admired wooded four-acre property just across from the Golden Gate Bridge, north of San Francisco. It boasted views of the Pacific Ocean and even had a few old-growth redwood trees still standing in the yard. The Cliff House, as they named it, gave Duncan and Blythe just the right amount of privacy and rejuvenation they needed at the end of their always-intense workdays, where they were changing the world in the tech industry decision by decision—innovating, transforming, and dominating. The custom-built house was a pre-child project that had brought them together.

Kora immediately gravitated to their outside space. She was calmest when Blythe walked her around the property. As she grew, she toddled around and quickly got acquainted with the ten different species of oaks, fiddlehead ferns, and smooth-barked madrones on the property. There were 132 steps made from old railroad ties hand dug into the ledge that ended on the sand of the beach below. Kora spent much of her childhood with windblown sandy hair, playing on the beach. The waves were heavy and loud, smacking the beach, which was coarse gray sand made up of millions of tiny pebbles. But in winter, the force of the ocean would churn up sand from other beaches and the deeper parts of the sea, in a much bigger grade of stone.

Blythe called Kora her nature girl. It was almost impossible to get her to wear shoes, or clothes for that matter, on a warm day. Kora was almost always outside playing, building shelters with sticks, collecting worms, talking to birds, making mud cakes, and picking flowers and arranging them into artwork. She was happiest playing alone or with her dog, Zuma, a cute, spunky, perfect-size curly-haired dog. There was nothing better for her than being out in nature and immersed in her imagination.

Kora was in middle school before she agreed to her first sleepover. Blythe convinced her it might be a good adventure to invite Maxine, a girl from her class, to spend the night. Kora didn't particularly like or not like Maxine, but their parents were friends who were trying to make their kids friends. Mom-instigated friendship only works for so many years. Kora reluctantly accepted the playdate sleepover but was pretty sure that Maxine would not want to do the kinds of things Kora did.

Kora had thought they could play a board game, but her friend wanted to watch a movie on the enticing extra-large TV that covered the entire wall of the living room. Blythe was in favor of the movie, as she knew that the kids would be hypnotized and quiet for almost two full hours and she would not be called upon for that entire time.

Kora and Maxine piled onto the long, comfy brown leather couch and cuddled underneath a handmade afghan blanket that was the warmest and fuzziest of all. Kora's mom hooked them up with bowls of buttery popcorn with pink salt and maple syrup. And, as if she were waving a magic wand that would put the kids into a trance, Kora's mom aimed the clicker at the TV to turn on the movie. As soon as the intro credits rolled, the adults, both Duncan and Blythe, disappeared to different rooms to try and get some things accomplished.

Maxine asked Kora to turn up the volume when the dialogue began.

Kora called out, "Mom? Could you turn it up for us, please?" But her mom didn't respond.

Kora had noticed that the remote controls and appliances tended to act funny when she used them, so she suggested that Maxine adjust the volume—"So you can get it just how you like it." Maxine said her fingers were too buttery from the popcorn.

Kora placed her bowl of popcorn carefully on the side table, wiped her hands on one of the cotton napkins Blythe had provided, and disentangled herself from the afghan. She walked to the TV to adjust it manually using the few buttons hidden behind the little secret plastic door on the frame.

But when she made contact with the Volume Up button, the TV sparked, zapped, flashed, and began to smoke.

A small flame ignited behind the TV, started burning the cords, and soon grew bigger. The girls screamed. The adults came running. Blythe rushed the girls outside and tried to calm them while Duncan called 911. The girls were freaked. Kids are mesmerized by fire (who doesn't love to roast marshmallows around one and listen to the crackling in a fireplace?), but untamed fire is scary and traumatizing. Kora and Maxine had seen the sudden power and strength of the flame and its ability to spread quickly and unpredictably. To be so close to an unwanted fire made them realize how quickly flames could get out of control, and they saw that there was no limit to the power fire could generate or what it would consume.

Investigations into the cause of the fire in the Greenways' home were inconclusive. It was assumed that some recent renovations and the electrical wiring on the new home theater must not have been up to code.

Kora knew the fire was truly an accident, but she was also strongly aware that she created the spark that set the TV on fire. The last thing she wanted to do was hurt anyone—or her home. She did not dare to tell her parents of the power surge that came from her and caused the damage. She thought they would punish her or send her back, as irrational as that might be. But she was also distressed and wanted to know where the heck that power spark came from.

Kora didn't really know how to articulate what she was feeling, so the next morning as she ate her homemade yogurt, she blurted out, "Mom, I think I have something in me."

Blythe looked up from the houseplants she was watering. "What do you mean, honey?"

"I feel . . . different. I wonder if there's something about me that's not the same as most people. Do you think it's because I'm adopted? Do you know anything about my real parents?"

"Kora, you know that your dad and I are your real parents. You're a Greenway, all the way, sweetie, like it or not."

"Mom . . ."

Blythe gave Kora a little squeeze. "Well, you were born in Ecuador. At the orphanage there, some of the staff told us they thought you might have been born in the rainforest. We all agreed that it made sense such a beautiful baby would come from such a beautiful place!"

"Mom! Sheesh . . ." Kora blushed but squeezed her mom back. "I just feel like I'm wired differently or something. I don't think Maxine or the other kids at school feel the same way I do inside."

"Kora, honey, maybe it's puberty! You must be blossoming into womanhood. Remember how I was telling you how our bodies change, and sometimes our emotions and our bodies feel—"

"MOM! I don't mean hormones!"

"Well, what do you mean?" Blythe was genuinely concerned. She'd never heard Kora sound this upset.

"What if it's something from my biological parents that makes me different?" A tear trickled down Kora's cheek.

"Sweetie, I get it. You'd like to know more about your biological parents to know more about yourself. But there wasn't any information about your birth parents from the adoption agency. I'm so sorry. I wish I could give you what you want. But I want you to know: whoever you came from, you are made of love and kindness, and you will always be loved . . . by me!" She smothered Kora in a huge bear hug to show her devotion to the only daughter she had, the person she loved most in the world.

From her mom's embrace, Kora said in a muffled voice, "The TV, the fire—that was me, Mom. A spark came out of my hands. This energy in me, is it evil? Is it good? I want to know what it is, why it's in me, how I got it, and what I'm supposed to do with it." She was overwhelmed by how hard she had been trying to hide the energy in her body that had become destructive.

Blythe tried to soothe even while she worked to comprehend what her daughter meant about energy. This seemed like more than just auras and moods, but how can one know what it feels like inside someone else's skin? "Everyone's energy is different, Kora. You have to embrace it, manage it, and one day celebrate it. As you grow up, you'll learn all about yourself and your energy, and you'll know your challenges also build your character. Your energy will teach you and lead you to do great things."

That made Kora feel good for a second, but she still secretly wanted to know more about her past, her birth parents, and this strange feeling of heat and emotion inside of her that was now coming out in the form of fire. She felt she couldn't fully step into understanding who she was until she knew her own history, and it ate away at her. A day did not go by without her daydreaming about her origin story. She had fantasized about a few potential scenarios and liked the stories she told herself about her beginnings, but she wanted the real story.

It was clear to Blythe that Kora was struggling on many levels. It was hard enough navigating through the changes of becoming a teenager without adding in weird fire tendencies, feeling out of control, being adopted, having a different color skin than her family, and all the other insecurities of growing and changing into an identity—plus so many holes in the story of who Kora was and how she fit in. It was too much piling up, and Blythe wondered if Kora was crying out for help by setting things on fire.

Blythe realized that she needed to reach out and get some kind of help for Kora.

CHAPTER 4

A LITTLE HELP, PLEASE

CALIFORNIA

One remnant from her corporate win-at-all-costs life before Kora was that Blythe did not hesitate to find her daughter the help she needed. Blythe knew darn well that her parenting skills were not sufficient to help herself and Kora through these times on their own. Raising Kora was the most important job in her life, so she needed to figure out how to do that best, which included finding and using every resource. Being well into her forties, Blythe had finally figured out how to ask for help and get help, and had no insecurities about it. She might not be the expert in every field, but she was very good at finding them. "That's what specialists are for!" was her mantra.

Blythe knew there were a million therapists out there. You didn't want to choose one out of thin air, but Dr. Marshall was someone a friend, who was a therapist herself, recommended. Kora knew she could use someone and was willing to see what talk therapy had to offer, so she agreed to go and was grateful her mom was trying to help her. This was a good first step.

Kora and her mom sat uncomfortably on an overstuffed couch, sucked into the pillows like they were stuck in a hug they didn't want in the first place. The couch was so plush, neither of them could reach the ground with their feet. They fell into each other from the center seam.

A perfect stranger sat across from them, evaluating Kora. On the wall behind him were diplomas made into plaques from prestigious schools like Columbia, UC Berkeley, and Vanderbilt. Dr. Marshall was a short, round, bald man with large circular wire-rimmed glasses who was dressed by his wife down to his leather loafers and a pink polo shirt with khaki pleated pants. He started by saying, "We are all best served if I can get accurate information about your current life situation. . . ." And he then broke into the questioning like it was a job interview, but of emotions. He had the backstory already from Blythe about why they wanted the session—out of concern that Kora might be starting fires.

He was a get-to-the-point kind of therapist and didn't take much time for warm-up or chitchat, since they only had an hour and the clock was ticking. He began an intense interrogation without much establishment of trust or two-way communication.

"Do you ever hurt your dog when you're upset?"

Offended, Kora answered promptly. "No, that is awful. I would never think to do that. I love Zuma and would do anything to protect him." She was more than a little shocked, and realized she needed to clarify for the doctor. "Look, I don't *want* to mess things up, I'm not trying to."

He moved on to the next question on his intake form. "Overall, how would you describe your mood?"

Kora felt her heart rate elevate. "Not so happy . . . kinda lost?" Her voice cracked, and she ended in a question, unsure how she was supposed to respond. Her mom reached over to grab her hand reassuringly.

Dr. Marshall scribbled some notes down. Kora really didn't like how that made her feel, as if she were at some audition or test. She felt like she was being judged, and she wanted to know what he was noting down each time after she spoke. Then the doctor asked her mother some more questions. There was no beating around the bush with this guy. "Do you feel like your child poses a threat of imminent danger to herself or others?" he asked Blythe.

Kora's mom did not want to say anything that could be held against them. "Well, no. I don't feel she has any bad intentions. We just know she struggles with some reactions."

Eyes and interrogation shifted back to Kora. "If you had a magic wand, what positive change would you like to see happen in your life?"

Kora thought deeply. "Hmm, I don't know. I just really want to figure out why I feel this energy inside of me—why I have it and where it comes from." Why did she act and react in a certain way? Kora was not going to offer up that she could fire lightning bolts out of her fingertips. She knew that it would not go over well if she revealed this information.

There were longer-than-usual awkward moments of silence as they sat in the tiny room that kind of smelled of pleather. Kora evaluated every touch of attempts at interior design in the room and wondered why that ceramic bowl was put there on the table, and what the little sculpture was about on the shelf, and why he chose that random framed photo of a covered bridge for this space.

Blythe, who had been in her share of therapists' offices over the years, was feeling fidgety as she crossed and uncrossed her legs, trying to get comfortable even though it was Kora, not her, digging deep into Freudian motivations. Kora finally got her legs into a comfortable cross-legged position on top of the saggy couch cushion, not shy to gently defy etiquette to finally feel grounded. Her mother wished she could take off her serious mom heels and do the same.

"If you are purposefully damaging things around you, Kora, you may have a degree of an anger management problem," Dr. Marshall intoned.

He gave Kora a yellow handout of some basic beginning steps to managing anger:

1. *Take deep breaths.*
2. *Wait 10 seconds before you respond.*

He also recommended that she start meditating and suggested a medication that could help smooth out Kora's heated moods and give her better focus. This was just the Greenways' first stop to see if they could get any help, support, or guidance in the weird issues Kora was experiencing, but it was clear the connection with this therapist was not great.

Blythe and Kora didn't buy it. They both knew that Kora had energy inside her that had something to do with electronic disruption. Her wristwatches never lasted; when she walked by radios, they went to static; any battery-operated device seemed to malfunction after she held it; and now she was noticing sparks when she touched anything that plugged in. She was already trying to control it, and she meant no harm. Kora had been kind of excited when she'd been watching the movie with her friend, but she wasn't overwhelmed or angry in a way that should have turned a spark into a flame.

Both Kora and her mom felt that this psychologist was way off, tossing out a diagnosis without actually knowing the whole story. On the surface, yes, it might sound like Kora had issues moderating her moods, but they both knew it was something different. Something weirder than heated emotion was going on. They silently respectfully disagreed with his diagnosis and declined the offer of medication. Blythe extended her arm, covered in all sorts of beaded bracelets, and offered a farewell handshake. They thanked the therapist for his time, and they left the office as fast as they could escape.

"All I got to say is that was a bunch of BS!" Blythe whispered to Kora, and she rarely swore. Kora didn't feel angry at all; the fires were starting because Kora herself was a little spark. At that moment Blythe knew it was time to turn to an alternative approach.

CHAPTER 5

MARTIAL ARTS & MAKING FRIENDS

CALIFORNIA

It was Ms. Piper, Kora's karate teacher, who officially explained Kora's energy gift. Concerned that Kora preferred solitary play more than being with other kids her age, and thinking of ways to burn through the energy that Kora said made her feel uncomfortable, Blythe sensed that Kora could use both a teacher and an individualized sport. So, Kora's mom brought her to a Kenpo karate studio that had a reputation for excellence, even though Blythe herself knew nothing about the world of martial arts.

The karate studio was in a normal strip mall, with a convenient parking lot in front shared with the frozen yogurt place and a dry cleaner on the other side. The entire studio was one large padded rectangular room. The owner, Andrea Piper, apparently held a stratospheric ninth-degree black belt ranking, one that very few women in the world held. But she did not hang her credentials on the wall or her sleeve; they were just stripes on her well-worn belt, which she tied closer to her left hip, as was traditional since she was a woman.

Ms. Piper kept her studio Zen and simple, with the intention of sharing karate with willing and motivated young students interested in knowing the martial arts intimately. She taught in order to provide her students with the skills needed to succeed in life, focusing on lessons about confidence, focus, self-esteem, respect, and physical well-being through movement and self-defense.

Kora's mom was impressed by the only message on the wall. It read, "Kenpo Karate teaches the art of self-defense, instilling self-respect, self-discipline, honor, courage, and perseverance in its students, who span the globe." Blythe knew this was what she wanted her daughter to learn. She thought this approach might be exactly what Kora needed to help her feel more grounded in herself. And right away, Kora felt at home.

Ms. Piper was a badass in her *gi*, the white karate uniform she lived and worked in. If she were in street clothes, it would be hard to know her body was a weapon, since she looked like an ordinary thirty-two-year-old woman going out for errands. She had jaggedly cut curly blond hair and the frame of a midsize soccer player. Her strength came from within somewhere, as her muscles didn't advertise great power, but she was a gentle force of nature. She was soft spoken, humble, and very kind spirited, but out on the mats her *kiai*, the sound she made with each striking move, was loud and echoing and sounded like it should come out of the mouth of a much larger person.

Kora started in classes with other twelve-year-olds, but Ms. Piper immediately identified Kora's extraordinary abilities. Ms. Piper had known other special people with this high level of energy, and she was delighted that someone with these powers had walked into her studio one day with her mom. Once, Ms. Piper had been thrown across a room with a flick of the finger by her grandmaster teacher and was humbled by the power. She spent the rest of her life studying the martial art of how to do that herself. Kora was already there—without ever having one lesson. She had the power without even trying.

Ms. Piper knew her job was not to get Kora to have more power, rather to help her train this force—to tame it and use it for good. She would never have a student like this again, so she was dedicated to teaching Kora all that she knew about this type of energy work. When Ms. Piper first explained Kora's energy to her, Kora was incredulous.

"Really? This is a *good* thing? That feels hard to believe, Ms. Piper. Because I feel like Dr. Destruction. Everything I touch! Did my mom tell you about the time I started a fire in our house by accident?"

"No, but I get it, Kora. I know only a few masters of *chi gung* who have trained in the ancient practice of coordinating one's posture and movement, along with breath and meditation, to achieve a balance of the life energy circulating through their body. This power is what you have flowing through you. We all do. But yours seems to be a special high-level force that includes heat, light, and electromagnetic energy. I will teach you how to control it, but it takes great effort. Masters of this energy that you have can bend a metal pole by barely touching it, because they've learned to use this ancient method."

Kora confided in Ms. Piper, "I feel like I'm a volcano, and I'm scared that I am going to erupt out of nowhere! I hate living like this. I'm always wondering when and where it's going to boil up. I just want to be normal and not think about this all the time."

Ms. Piper told her, "Like anyone, you'll just have to learn how to live with who you are. But I can help you turn this power into something you can manage, and beyond that, be proud of and use to your advantage!"

"OK, but why do I have to work on this so hard just to be normal?" Kora was surprised how comfortable she instantly felt with Ms. Piper, who seemed to be the first person to see all of who she was and understand.

"What is 'normal,' anyway, Kora? Instead of trying so hard to be like others, why don't you try hard to be yourself? This is part of you, you may as well accept it."

Ms. Piper realized that Kora felt more stable and centered when she was outside, so they started doing private sessions on the beach in front of the Greenways' home. The energy work they did looked effortless but required high focus. Kora and Ms. Piper warmed up with push hands, moving the energy back and forth between them, as if they were passing back and forth an invisible ball of fire that neither of them desired to hold on to. To the untrained eye, it looked like they were just trying to push each other over, but they were practicing an ancient Hsing I martial art that harnessed enough power to be deadly. Either one of them could throw anyone across the beach, sending them flying from one touch of this brewed-up energy, but they didn't. They just danced in the energy of the moment, exhilarated by the pure potential they were playing with together.

Between training sessions, Kora would practice by herself near the water. She could pass energy from hand to hand, feeling the flow and controlling it. Sometimes it sparked, but most of the time it felt like an almost-pleasant buzzing and warmth. While she practiced, Zuma, her ever-faithful companion, would take turns chasing seagulls, jumping at the lapping waves, and lying down nestled in the sand, feeling the heat of the sun (or maybe the heat coming from Kora), following her with his puppy eyes as he watched his master train to be a martial arts master.

One day, while Kora was focused on her energy practice, a boy her age wandered the beach. He carried two trash bags in one hand and a grabber in the other. He was putting recyclables in one bag and trash in the second. Because he had been scanning the sand for litter and she was so intent on trying to pass energy up and down between her hands rather than back and forth, from side to side, the boy got pretty close to Kora before either of them realized—close enough that Zuma wagged his tail and gave a little hello bark.

Bodi had seen Kora on the beach from time to time when he was surfing, and he had watched her from his board. This day, suddenly finding himself in speaking distance, he finally spoke up. "Hi! I've seen you around before, and I wanted to ask you, are you doing some kind of martial art?"

Kora always got shy when people addressed her directly, especially about things that related to her power. But this boy looked nice. He had been cleaning up the beach, and Zuma seemed to trust him, so, uncharacteristically, Kora replied. "Yeah, something like that. Chi gung."

"Oh, yeah, my dad is into that stuff."

"Does your dad practice martial arts, or does he just like to watch kung fu movies?"

"Um, I think my dad actually does it. He lives in Costa Rica, though. I haven't seen him since I was five, but my mom told me that he was into it. I don't know much about it, but it looks really cool. I'd like to learn it someday. By the way, I'm Bodi. Nice to meet you both." He addressed Kora, then smiled down at Zuma.

"Zuma, go make friends," Kora commanded with a grin. Exceptionally loyal dog that he was, Zuma had been watching and assessing this boy, but he liked him right away. Zuma could sense that Bodi was not threatening in the least bit to his Kora. The dog accepted the command, got up and shook the sand off, and was the perfect ice-breaker. Zuma skipped over to Bodi, with front paws excitedly raised to a potential new friend. He leaned his body on Bodi's leg to accept a few pats and then rolled upside down for a long belly rub, unknowingly becoming the bridge that led Bodi and Kora to become friends.

CHAPTER 6

ACCOMMODATIONS

CALIFORNIA

If there was one thing that Kora's mom was really good at, it was cutting through bureaucracy to get her way. Knowing that touching electronics was a problem for her daughter, Blythe was determined to figure out a work-around. Kora's electrical power couldn't constantly be disrupting the wired world around her, which everyone except her depended on. So when she needed to get Kora excused from touching electronics at school, Blythe came to the middle school on a mission.

Kora and her mom both knew they had to get some kind of accommodation to avoid any other potential blowups, fires, sparks, or strange, potentially harmful electrical snafus happening in school. But, of course, Blythe couldn't just say, "My daughter has electrical problems." That wouldn't make any sense to most people. Instead, after much planning, Blythe went in to talk to the principal, bringing Kora with her. She also brought a note she got her ophthalmologist friend to write stating that Kora had a negative response to computers' blue lights, calling it something official like Computer Vision Syndrome. Blythe argued that the school needed to protect Kora from vision deterioration by keeping her away from computers.

That was how Kora's mother convinced the principal to write a 504 special accommodation learning plan saying that Kora needed to go totally old-school in her classes, making it official policy that Kora would not and could not be expected to do any academic work on computers. This had never been requested or granted before, but somehow, Blythe had come up with a way to keep Kora and everyone around her safe by making sure she didn't have to interact with technology directly.

They left the office—with the accommodation signed, sealed, and delivered—and let the heavy door slam behind them. They wanted to high-five each other, but settled with sharing beaming smiles. Blythe would always tell Kora, "It's my job as your mom to be on your team! And if I can make your life easier, I will do whatever I can. 'Cause life can be hard sometimes, for all of us." Their team had scored a big victory that day.

They walked out of the administrative part of the school to return Kora to her classroom—just in time for art. Bodi was sitting outside the nurse's office in one of those uncomfortable hard blue plastic school chairs fastened onto its frame with big, cold silvery bolts. The boy was looking kind of gray. Kora remembered him from the beach, but he wasn't looking as curious and full of life as he had that day. He slumped in the chair, a bit defeated by his own body.

Kora waved to him, and said a simple "Hi!"

He replied, "Oh, hi! I remember you, Kora, the Zen master from the beach." His body still slouched, but a little color was coming back into his face.

"Well, not really . . . Are you OK? You don't look so hot."

While Kora and Bodi struck up a conversation, Blythe blew an air-kiss to Kora and multitasked as she walked out of the school building, texting Duncan about their win with the principal. He didn't really understand Kora's need to avoid technology, but as long as Blythe was handling everything, he wasn't concerned. His work was stressful, and he needed to focus on it, so he just replied with a thumbs-up.

Bodi responded to Kora, a bit embarrassed, but comfortable enough to share with this friendly girl. "Yeah, I'm fine. . . . I will be fine! I just had a little asthma attack. No biggie, it happens every once in a while. The nurse just wants to watch me for a hot sec . . . but I'm all good. Thanks to my handy friend, my inhaler!"

"Oh, good. I'm glad you're OK." And naturally, Kora sat in one of the hard blue chairs set up for the next ill kid, and she just chilled with

Bodi, like a good friend would do, until he looked stable enough to stand on his own two feet.

CHAPTER 7

BLACKOUT

CALIFORNIA

Kora had learned to hide her differences from most people. But what some folks shamed her for, her best friend, Bodi, liked most about her. It was hard being a little different, especially at that age. Who doesn't want to be accepted, and for middle schoolers, who doesn't love devices? Only Kora. Plain and simple, when Kora and Bodi hung out, they were hanging out together. She wasn't transfixed, staring into a screen or interacting with someone not physically in front of her. Bodi appreciated her authentic presence when he was with her and enjoyed the conversation and time they spent together without distraction.

She and Bodi became pretty good surfers, often hitting the beach together. She liked learning at school, and also loved biking and exploring the natural environment around her whenever she could. But sometimes, her body gave her startling reminders that she was at her best when life was simple and she could be in the present moment.

On Kora's thirteenth birthday, after a special birthday dinner of veggie plop, as her mom called Kora's favorite stir-fried veggies over rice, it was time for presents. Kora had already planted her birthday tree with her parents earlier. The birthday tree planting was a tradition her mom had started on her first birthday at the Cliff House. Kora now had her own small orchard in her backyard because of it, some fruiting trees, some conifers, and other exotic deciduous trees suitable for their climate. Each time she planted a tree, it made her feel like an earth guardian.

Kora had enjoyed digging and planting with her parents (and Zuma had liked it, too), but now she was dreading the attention around unwrapping her final birthday gift. She had a feeling she knew what it was. Her dad thought that he was going to get the "You are the greatest dad in the world" treatment by giving her a very expensive piece of technology that any kid would die for. Kora was worried she was going to disappoint him.

Zuma sat himself down right next to Kora, as usual, always aware of where she was in proximity to him. She stroked the whole side of his body, which was reliably calming to her. She suddenly felt weird, and an unpleasant, familiar sensation flooded her body: shaking, sweating, heart racing, slight headache forming. Kora carefully pulled the stiff wrapping paper from around the beautifully engineered sturdy rectangle cardboard box.

"You are the luckiest kid. All the tech blogs say this phone is the *best*. It just came out, and it was very expensive, so don't lose it or break it!" Duncan said.

Kora had to fake her excitement because she wanted her parents to feel that she was appreciative and grateful. She smiled and said, "Thank you, Dad. I don't think I should have such a fancy thing." She held the box gently in her palms as if it were a fragile kitten who was already starting to purr.

Duncan insisted, "Try it out. You are going to be blown away! It has face recognition to unlock it. I preloaded some apps on there I thought you would love, and now that you're thirteen, you can start doing some social media. You can connect with all the kids from school. Come on, K—fire it up!"

Kora hesitated. She was scared to free it from the box. She was already feeling heat and humming vibrations in her hands that weren't related to the digging she had done to plant her birthday tree. Kora feared what would happen if she got any closer to the device. She had been deliberately avoiding these types of electronics for years now, without ever really explaining why to her dad. Blythe understood that Kora needed be tech-free, but even she had been unsure how to tell Duncan the reasons behind it.

Kora had been noticing more electrical problems lately. Bulbs would constantly blow out in her light fixtures in her room, breakers had to be reset in the house almost every week, and the clicker to the TV had started to smoke more than once, which really scared her, so she stopped touching it altogether. The appliances in her house were under constant repair. She had noticed even more surges in her energy output. Was puberty making everything worse? She had an out-of-body feeling at times. Her whole being seemed overly electrical, even with Ms. Piper's practice to control it.

Already her hands were shaking, and she began to sweat from her armpits. Kora sensed that she might have the opposite of the Midas touch, that instead of everything she touched turning to gold, everything she touched sparked and got electrified. She did not like the aggressive electrical pulse that seemed to charge through her body without her control, and she feared she was going to foul things up.

Kora had wanted an easel for outdoor painting for her birthday, or she would have even loved a houseplant for her room, or a cool new leash for Zuma . . . but her dad had gotten her a phone instead. A first phone was practically an American rite of passage because it meant more freedom. Some parents even believed that a phone was necessary for a healthy modern social life. She'd been able to hold out this long, but her dad thought he was doing her a favor.

"Check out some of the cool apps. You can see how far you ride your bike every day if you want! Or there's another one, if you hear a song you like, it tells you who the artist is." Her dad grabbed the charger and connected it to the wall. "Let's make sure it's all charged up. Mom and I had it wrapped and waiting for a few weeks, so the battery could be low."

He kept urging her to engage with the phone. She had a deep-down instinct to not pick it up. But he looked so hopeful. . . .

The moment Kora's finger softly touched the outside edge of the device, an electrical pulse overloaded the circuitry in the whole house. The power jolt scared her. She felt the electrical shock jump right out of her fingertips, but nobody else in the room witnessed the spark. The house went dark.

"Goddamn it all, I can't believe this, the power is out!" her dad said. No bars, no internet. The modem was down. In Duncan's world, they

had been thrown into a full-blown emergency. He tried various functions on his phone to make contact with the web, the outside world
. . . nothing. He frantically checked the light switches. The time on
the microwave oven had disappeared; buttons did not make reassuring
beeps. There would be no toasting, no blending, and most tragically, no
autodripping coffee. No music to calm the nerves.

"Nothing is working!" Her dad's emotions escalated to next-level
panic as he ran around the house checking everything that was plugged
in but not performing. It was invisible, yet systemic to the whole network, the brains of the smart house.

"Wait, the neighbors have lights! It's just our house, not a neighborhood power outage!" Duncan deduced after half an hour of frantically
racing around the house trying to fix something he had no control over.
It called for exploratory surgery in the walls to diagnose why the whole
electrical system was shot. The mysterious short circuit somehow
affected all the wiring, singeing every conductor that wove through the
walls like a loose-knit sweater. The lifeline of energy through the veins
of the house had been halted by Kora's touch.

The shutoff made Duncan progressively more panicked as the minutes of dysfunction ticked by. It was rare to ever be out of range these
days. Access to charging and electricity was as reliable as the family
dog, ready to go at any moment of the day or night. Nothing affects life
in the twenty-first century more than a power outage.

"Maybe turn it off and then turn it on at the main circuit breaker,
and let it sit for a count of twenty this time. Sometimes powering off
is a good way to reboot." Kora's mom tried to reassure him. "Duncan,
just take a deep breath. You have lived without a cell phone before.
Remember, when we were kids before the internet and cell phones
were even invented? You'll be alright for a few hours until we get it
figured out."

Kora noticed her dad's insecurities. He was acting like taking away
his Wi-Fi was like snatching a baby's blanket before bedtime. Duncan
was disconnected and would do anything to get that connection again.
Kora wished he wanted to connect with her instead of with his phone.
But he was clearly in the middle of a full-fledged meltdown.

To him, the loss of power felt like he went from living in the most
innovative smart house to living in a tent, since they were unable to

use any of their modern conveniences. To be honest, he hadn't done anything less luxurious than glamping with full Wi-Fi and solar electricity in decades. He had good reasons for that.

Blythe wanted to help calm Duncan but also wanted him to just accept life without electricity for the rest of the night. It was already 7:00 p.m., and they could deal with it tomorrow. Kora was so excited to go off-line for the night—it was the greatest birthday present she could imagine. And she was getting her mom fired up to settle in and unplug from it all, too. Why not treat themselves to that carefree feeling of a slower pace for a few hours?

Kora said, "Let's pretend we are at your summer camp, Mom—the one you went to as a kid that you tell me about all the time. Maybe you can even bust out the guitar! Can we have a campfire outside? Tell ghost stories?"

Blythe gathered all the candles she could find in the house, most of them fancy and never used before, and set them up in the living room. Kora was allowed to light a few candles by herself for the first time. When her mom taught her how to use a match, she loved that fire at her fingertips. It felt like magic, and the flame hypnotized her. For more than an hour, Kora was entertained by the dancing firelight and its glow, and she focused on that as Duncan continued to escalate into a near panic attack. Then she got out the big wooden chessboard with the hand-carved stone pieces that Blythe and Duncan were given as a wedding gift but seldom used.

"Anyone want to play?"

"Not now, Kora! Can't you see that we are still in a crisis?" her dad said frantically.

To Kora, the "crisis" felt more like a retreat. She liked the real, the simple, the basic, the moment, and had always craved a slower life. She was happy that the power outage meant a pause of the treadmill the whole family had been running on nonstop.

Duncan raced around the house flicking every switch and checking every appliance. Kora stayed quiet and out of the way in hopes that he wouldn't realize she was to blame.

"You have got to be kidding me!" her dad shouted. "How can this happen after all the money we just paid to make this a smart house? Nothing is smart here if there is no power!"

"It's going to be OK, Duncan, these things happen. We'll get it back up and running soon," Kora's mom said, knowing that there was nothing she could say when he got into one of these states. Ultimately, he knew calming techniques, but he refused to tap into them at times like this.

"In the meantime, it's still Kora's birthday, and we can still manage to have some fun. Maybe something simpler than chess? We can finally play one of those board games that have been sitting in this closet forever." She swung the cabinet doors open and gazed in with excitement. "Clue? Life? Trivial Pursuit?"

"Yes! Can you teach me to play Othello?" Kora said with a grin.

Duncan continued pacing around the house and on the deck with one arm outstretched like the Statue of Liberty, trying to see if he could get some bars on his phone to appear. Kora noticed that each piece of technology that couldn't perform for her dad made him even more anxious, while it made her feel more relaxed and freer. But, of course, she would never share this. It felt like yet another way she was a complete opposite of the rest of her family.

Duncan stomped back into the living room. "I'm going to a hotel. I can get on the Wi-Fi there tonight."

"OK, you go ahead, honey," Blythe said. "Kora and I are going to stay and have a mother-daughter campout in the house for a special birthday!" She gave Duncan a reassuring kiss and patted him on the rear out the door, secretly happy to clear the uptight energy around the situation and excited to get to spend some time alone with her daughter.

Those became some of Kora's fondest memories of her mom, that night together when they had no distractions. It felt like time was standing still, and the world outside their four walls was insignificant. What was important was the present moment that they got to spend just being, without doing, because of the absence of the world of technology for the night. They both felt connected to be out of touch. It was a much-needed temporary pause from the fast pace of life. The evening was like a breath of fresh air.

"Can we make this another tradition, Mom? On my birthdays, we spend a night camping in our own house, turn off the electricity, and just be together?" Kora had never been backpacking before, but she guessed the back to basics of it was similar to what she was experiencing.

"I love that idea!" her mom said, feeling more relaxed than she had in months.

"I didn't mean for this to happen, but I'm kind of glad it did," Kora admitted.

CHAPTER 8

PRACTICING WITH POWER

CALIFORNIA

As years passed, to Kora, it felt like a full-time job working to manage her power and lead a healthy life as a teenager. She kept her "gift" to herself and made sure not to flaunt it or use it for aggression. But it was hard. Nobody except Ms. Piper understood the work she had to put in every day.

After one particularly difficult session when Kora was sixteen, Ms. Piper said, "You have learned how to manage your power. I know it takes constant work to control, but really, everyone must learn how to have control in their life. Discipline is a muscle. All people have to find control over the tendencies that could eventually do them harm." She paused, giving Kora a meaningful look.

"People recovering from alcoholism have to work every day to make sure they don't reach for a drink when things get hard. Those with a gambling addiction need to work hard to make sure they don't throw all of their money away. Everyone who's addicted to overeating has to find the power to eat healthfully. Life is full of distractions. Every day we are faced with choices, and it takes great skill to be able to guide your life instead of sitting back and having things just happen to you. You are learning this."

Ms. Piper and Kora were practicing on the beach in front of Kora's house. It was a clear and crisp windy day. It looked like Kora was slowly moving her hands up and down in front of her body as she breathed into imaginary inflatable balls she was holding in front of her, but with the rise and fall of Kora's hands, she was stalling the waves in the ocean before her as they broke—for one brief moment. It was a challenging skill only mastered by an exceptional few. Kora watched her action in disbelief but was also excited by the power she was harnessing.

Ms. Piper taught her another exercise of sifting sand through her hands. Kora had always been fascinated by sand. She could look deep into every grain and see history, a story, a piece of the universe. It amazed her that, together, the sand made an entire beach, but individually, a grain was just one speck alone in the world . . . like her. Kora grabbed handfuls of sand, focused on each particle in her hand, and passed the sand from one palm to the other.

"Like this?" She looked for guidance from her teacher.

So much of the teaching was nonverbal. Ms. Piper mirrored the motion, dropping the sand from one hand to the next.

Kora rubbed her hands full of sand together to heat it and took a few focused breaths into them. She threw the sand piles in her palms up into the air, but two solid rocks dropped to the ground, transformed, reconstituted back to pre-eroded form.

Ms. Piper tried not to get too excited about her student mastering another of these ancient skills, but it was quite extraordinary energy work.

"You can spin into the negative or choose to see it as a positive, Kora. . . . You get to choose. For an athlete, or a master at anything, for that matter, the training is never over; it is always a work in progress." Ms. Piper had realized early on that it was Kora's mind she had to train more than her physical ability.

"I still feel like a hazard, though," Kora admitted.

Despite the cool trick with the sand, at that moment, Kora had the "why me" blues. The pep talk from her teacher hadn't landed in the intended uplifting way. Kora could come up with a whole list of hard struggles and challenges in her life that she already had to deal with, like sticking out as the brown kid in a white family, being introverted, not knowing where she came from and where she belonged. She also struggled with being short, not having boobs, and living in a digital world that she refused to engage with.

"You are just wired differently, Kora. You feel things differently. You are more tuned in, shall we say, than others. You have a gift here. It is not an impediment."

Kora sighed and picked up another pile of sand, then let it sift through her fingers.

Ms. Piper bowed and slapped the sides of her legs to dismiss the training. Kora did the same, the traditional sign of respect when training in martial arts.

CHAPTER 9

A WORLD ON FIRE

CALIFORNIA

The town's two-tone emergency siren blared.

This was not the first mandatory evacuation Kora and her family had experienced since living in the Cliff House in Northern California. In Kora's sixteen years of life, there had been eleven calls of evacuation for brush fire, mudslide, flash flood, earthquake, and tsunami threats. As climate change got more real, the weather events became bigger and stronger. Floods and fires that used to have a historical pattern of once every fifty or one hundred years were becoming annual events.

It was always something. Living right on the coast came with frequent natural disasters. If you were a Californian in the twenty-first century, your go bag had to be packed, and your survival kits were ready in your house and your car. They said to pack the things you needed to live if evacuated for up to a week. That was just how it was if you lived in that zone, just like those who lived on the Gulf of Mexico knew they would be up against hurricanes that got stronger and stronger each year.

You learned to live with the constant threats in places where the forest was crispy dry and could go up like a tinderbox from the smallest spark. Rain was always a good thing, but residents also knew that the vegetation that grew healthy from the precipitation would also go dry at times, turn to tinder as undergrowth, and act as fuel if a spark did get loose.

Kora and Bodi had been walking on the beach when they heard the siren. Bodi's phone chimed in with an emergency alert right afterward. The sky changed from a plume to a blanket of smoke, and Bodi and Kora knew that they should get home. But maybe the beach was the safest place to be.

For a moment, they were stunned, as the enveloping smoke also had a way of clouding the mind. Kora knew this fire wasn't started by one of her sparks, for sure, and she felt relieved before the panic of another evacuation set in. It was reported that this particular fast-acting, overly hot wildfire had been started by a cigarette tossed from a moving car. It quickly grew to a wall of flames that started ripping through town.

Of course, as a kid, it had made Kora fearful when there was a call to evacuate. There had been some close calls, which kept her on high alert, but somehow these near misses made her parents less sensitive to the warnings. Blythe and Duncan seemed to become numb because, in the end, most of the events were not as dramatic as had been promised or predicted. But lately in California and other parts of the West, there had been wildfire after wildfire that wiped entire towns, neighborhoods, and landmarks off the map.

Kora would always have the feeling burned in her memory of panicked moments where she was supposed to grab her most-prized possessions and load them in the car to make a mad dash to somewhere far from where the fire raged. She knew all too well that in a state of fight or flight, you don't make the most rational or logical decisions. Last time she grabbed the succulent that lived on her desk, her journal, drawing pens, and Zuma on his leash, but she forgot the essentials like clothes and toiletries. No "thing" was as important to her as her dog, and as Zuma was loaded with her in the car, she was not concerned if the rest of the stuff burned. She knew that life was way more valuable than things.

Kora's parents became some of those stubborn residents who refused to evacuate because they didn't want to leave their pride-and-joy home, custom built to withstand category 5 wind conditions. They were overly confident because they had a high fireproof roof that they paid extra for. Like some other residents, they owned their own fire hose, as if Duncan were really going to stay and fight a fire. It made him feel good to have it, but they all knew he would probably be the first to abort if the flames came really close. But, these days, you had to defend your own. When the fires raged, there were not enough firefighters to go around.

They had been lucky. Their house had withstood and remained unscathed every time—so far.

Kora's mother got adrenaline from the crisis and often would drive out to the nearest burn to see for herself what was going on. It was so hard, even with the updates from Twitter and Cal Fire, to know what was really taking place nearby. Sometimes hearing it on the news or in the reports was not enough to understand what was happening just miles away, so she would go out. Kora hated this, and Duncan did, too, but there was no stopping Blythe. She would channel her storm chaser alter ego, and they just had to let her go.

Kora wished that her mom could just cuddle her in bed, stay home with her, and play board games. But some mama-bear instinct possessed Blythe to gather the data herself, and she would jump in her car. For some reason, Blythe loved the energy in the air, the wind, the heat, and the risk. While others ran the opposite direction, there was something in her that urged her closer to the danger. She would drive super close to the edge of the burn, as close as she could get to where the real firefighters had barricaded the roads, and personally ask the police and firefighters for the scoop, since she no longer trusted the news.

That day, on the beach, the sky was an apocalyptic gray, and the sun was blood orange, as if Bodi and Kora were on another planet. Bodi read Kora the emergency alert that came through on his cell phone. "Stage 4 evacuation in effect for the entire valley." Even though it was afternoon, there was a dusk feeling as if the sun were about to fade away.

Kora looked out in the direction of the original plume. She could see the flicker of red and orange flames on the distant hills, and knew it was bad. "Should we go home, or stay here?" Kora asked.

"Let me call my mom. I'll call your folks, too!" But Bodi's calls weren't going through. Texts weren't either. No one's were. The fire must have burned the cell towers and taken down the broadband. What good was a phone without a network?

They decided the best thing to do would be to stay put near the biggest body of water on earth. If they needed to jump in, they would.

Behind them, the sky was daunting. No blue was left to be seen, nor any color for that matter. Everything was muted and hazed. Kora and Bodi just hoped that their families were OK and that their folks weren't worrying too much about them. Being separated from family at a time like this could be scarier than the fire itself.

Kora was beginning to feel the smoke in the back of her throat. Each breath added to the slight headache that was developing, whether from the worsening air quality or the stress and tension, she couldn't tell. The outside temperature was heating up, adding to an already hot and uncharacteristically dry day on the coast. The fire was making its own weather system and was sucking out all humidity into a dry, toasty wind, helping the fire spread. They could see a wall of gray and black smoke now at the north edge of their town. It didn't take long for ash to begin to rain down, dusting a layer like snow on every surface. In addition to the evacuation siren's tones, they could hear fire sirens in the direction of downtown, which they both lived not too far from.

They knew that there were only two ways to evacuate the town, to the north or the south. Bodi and Kora wondered if there was even a chance of snuffing out the fire before it got out of control. Just then, they saw two scooper planes come flying low over the ocean, offshore from where they stood. It felt like bomber planes in war. A war against fire.

Bodi explained, "Oh, that's good! Those are firefighting airplanes, scooper aircraft. I heard each one can hold up to sixteen hundred gallons. Look, they are scooping up ocean water to drench the fire. That should help." He hoped to calm Kora, since he could tell she was starting to stress hard. Embers flew in the sky around them, drifting in the wind to the next roof, tree, or patch of vegetation. The fire was gaining and consuming fuel, acting like a monster gobbling up a village.

When they saw the brush on the bluff catch fire and had a view of actual blue and green flames, Bodi grabbed a surfboard that had been propped up, abandoned, by the seawall near the parking lot. They waded into the surf to both pile on the surfboard. Kora hopped on the board first, on her belly, and grabbed the rails. She grabbed Zuma by the collar as he loyally swam alongside and hoisted him up to the nose of the board. Bodi guided the board as far as he could while walking, until the sandy bottom disappeared. He slid on the end of the board and did the paddling to maneuver them all beyond the break, where they would stay in the water for most of an hour, as they watched fire rip through the beachfront properties. The water was cold, but their adrenaline kept them warm.

They saw the beach shack where they sometimes bought a cold drink go up in flames. They couldn't believe how fast the thing ignited, but at least they knew nobody was in the building, because they had gone by earlier and were bummed that nobody was in there to let them buy a cold ice tea.

Embers flew through the air like fireflies. The flames did not know or care what they would destroy next, they just drifted in the wind like a virus, their mere existence and mode of survival was to spread. The fire was closing in. But in the water, together, Bodi and Kora were safe, although incredibly scared.

"Bodi, how long can we stay in the water?"

"I surfed at this spot without a wetsuit and stayed in for two hours once. We are in a good place! I'd rather be here than there. . . ." He pointed to the land. "Fire can't get us here!" And then from the horizon, a small coast guard dinghy, with a few other survivors in it, approached, waving them to get in.

***

Kora's mother was counted as one of the forty-three people who died in that fire. The details of how she died were vague. Kora imagined the millions of scenarios of her mom's last thoughts, last breaths; it brought her nothing but horror, nightmares, and trauma. Search and rescue teams with sniffing dogs scoured neighborhoods and debris to see if they could find any remains. They warned that the fire was so hot, almost everything turned to ash.

Two whole towns were burned to the ground, essentially wiped off the map. There yesterday, gone today. All that was left was a burned-out skeleton of Kora's town. The Greenways' house partially burned, and the fire and smoke damage made it uninhabitable. Even if it had been unscathed, to Kora it wouldn't have felt like home without her mom. After too much loss to deal with, Kora and her dad had no choice but to move into a hotel in a nearby town for the time being.

Kora was in pure shock and could not comprehend how a weather event could change her life like that forever. She had a mom one moment and all was lost the next. *Why?* was all she could think. Kora could feel her electrical powers wanting to rage.

CHAPTER 10

LOSS AND
A CALL TO ACTION

CALIFORNIA

Much like the feeling of being so tired you could not sleep, at first Kora was so sad she could not cry.

Bodi went to the Greenways' temporary housing, a soulless, furnished business traveler suite in a sterile hotel, to console her the day after they escaped the fire. He came in with a hug, no words, because he didn't have any words of wisdom or experience in what she was going through. He knew that whatever he said could not ease any of the pain and heartache that she was feeling, but he also knew he could just be there, a shoulder, a friend.

Kora slumped into his strong chest and cried, finally. She had no words either. Something in her came unhinged. Her grief and confusion covered Bodi in the form of tears as Kora finally connected with the deep bellowing cries of all humanity. Bodi's embrace was the only thing holding her up at that moment, so she leaned in.

Finally, after many minutes, she spoke in between hyperventilating gasps. "How could Nature do this to my mom? It's not fair!"

Still, Bodi couldn't muster anything to say. He knew that his words were not going to make an impact now, that it was her time to speak.

"How could we let the world get so messed up that fires happen like this and wipe out whole towns and families?" she sobbed.

***

For weeks after the devastating loss of her mom, Kora was more angry than sad. She felt like she always had to be on the move, because if she stopped doing, the pain of losing her mom would flood in, like a mudslide that could bury people. She was haunted by a strange sense that she needed to act, to do something. She wanted to get vengeance, or reparation. She needed to blame. She needed to right a wrong. Kora wondered how she could ever recover.

Climate change killed her mom. Why wasn't anyone doing anything about this? Scientists had been publishing peer-reviewed science, describing why this happened again. But nobody was listening to scientists, and somehow their studies became controversial. People took sides, but Kora felt like she was living in a chasm of despair. It was a massive effort for Kora to get her powers under control during her grief. She took deep breaths to calm herself, but the fire that killed her mom burned hotter in her—in her heart, her being.

Kora essentially had to take care of herself as her dad continued to fall apart. She managed to get herself fed, and kept busy with school. Kora knew better than to discuss politics, spirituality, environmental concerns, or anything she was passionate about with her dad. Sometimes, emotionally, people are hanging on by a thread; it was invisible, but her dad's connection to people, friends, community, and work almost unraveled.

Duncan said out loud that he thought Kora not eating meat was just a way to be difficult, he felt her commitment to recycling was a waste of time, and he did not want to hear her thoughts on global warming and climate change. Kora had accepted that they were not cut from the same cloth, but she was still trying to find some connection since he was her only parent now. These outright denunciations of her principles cut deep.

Blythe's death had pulled Kora and her dad further apart instead of closer together, and a weird disconnect grew between them. Sometimes it felt like they were not even family anymore.

One night, Kora came back from hanging out at Bodi's trailer to what was now her "room" for who knew how long, in the two-bedroom suite. Duncan was facing the wall, oblivious to her, as he wrestled with some urgent call on his cell phone, which was tethered to the charger. He didn't even notice Kora enter the space, he was so deep into some problem-solving.

Kora was usually greeted by Zuma, who would whip around the corner to lick, wag, and lean against Kora every time they reunited. But today, when she could use that fuzzy salutation most, no Zuma.

"Dad, where is Zuma?" she asked with a sinking feeling.

"A hotel isn't a place for a dog to live. He was just too much for me to deal with right now, with all that is going on. I gave him to a guy who works for me. They have a few acres in San Rafael. The dog will be much happier there than living in a hotel. Who knows when we will be back in our real house—I'm on the phone with the good-for-nothing insurance company, again."

Kora could not believe her dad had said what he did, all without looking up, making eye contact, or even feeling bad about it.

"You gave my dog away? Without telling me?" She could instantly feel her energy rising. She was so close to destroying the whole hotel room and everything around her evil dad. "I can't believe you! That dog was all I had for family anymore."

"You still have me!" Kora's dad looked up, finally, with more pain in his expression than she expected. Her heart throbbed with compounded loss, broken but unmeltable.

"You do nothing for me! You don't understand me one bit, and I don't get you. I know you didn't want to adopt a kid in the first place. Well, guess what, you're stuck with me, Dad. You can't just pawn me off on a coworker with a bigger yard," she belted out as her face got red with anger.

She went off on him, for everything: the dog, her mom, his work, the state of the planet, and how he lived. . . . Her words gushed out in a torrent of pain until finally she had nothing more to give.

Kora turned her back on her dad and left to spend the night on Bodi's mom's couch. She was in no place to have a discussion. All she had to say was that her dad was ruining it all.

CHAPTER 11

AN AP ENVIRO EMERGENCY

CALIFORNIA

Kora had gone back to eating and sleeping at the hotel, but she and Duncan hadn't said more than a few sentences to each other since their flare-up. After all the silence at home, even the worst classes in school were a welcome escape.

Kora sat in the back corner of her AP Enviro class, trying to blend in with the wall paint. She loved the topic, but not the teacher. She was required to be in class physically, but mentally she was not there. Most of the time she tuned the teacher out and got everything she needed to know from the textbook that came with the course. It was reassuring to her to own a heavy four-inch-thick book with a stout cover, since almost every other class was computer heavy, and she always had to figure out her own way to get the information, if not by screen.

She was a hungry learner for topics that interested her, like climate science and political science, but mostly, she learned on her own through curiosity—and going through the bookshelf of yellow *National Geographic* magazines that she had been collecting since her grandma got her a subscription from the age when she could look at pictures and wonder about the world. That had been enough to inspire her for some time. It was a shame that this burned-out teacher, with his aggravating voice and greasy hair, tainted the whole learning experience for her.

Of course, Kora continued to learn about environmental science from current events every day outside of class. Even without a phone with news notifications, you couldn't avoid hearing about the next record-breaking hurricanes, droughts, sea level rise, floods, and melting glaciers. Wildfires.

Her teacher did not approach climate change with the urgency and significance she felt it required. Mr. Giles needed to be recycled, but he had five more years until his pension kicked in. So another round of students were stuck while he burned out, for another half decade, until he could exit into the sunset.

Kora was thinking about being in nature, and feeling the need to get out of the building as soon as possible, but, unlike rebellious students, she played by the rules and sat there. This was yet another day of Kora being checked out. The lectures weren't being transmitted into her brain; she was not following. The class might as well have been conducted in another language. She was there but not there. To shake off the stillness of sitting in a chair at school for so long, she daydreamed about jumping on her red cruiser mountain bike that was locked up outside the school and visualized herself pedaling so fast that the wind was pushing her hair behind her.

A squeaking chair pulled Kora out of her thoughts. She could tell that Mr. Giles had started off class that day already grumpy. He probably planned to have a quiet morning period where he could finish his entire coffee drink from yet another to-go paper cup while he administered yet another multiple-choice test. Maybe he just didn't feel like talking. Maybe that was why his voice sounded like *blah blah blah* instead of real words when he lectured. That made her tune him out even more.

Kora was probably the only kid in the school who turned in her homework handwritten on paper, since she avoided devices as if they were poison oak. She was still mindful to uphold her commitment not to touch them. Every day she was grateful for her mother's ability to get her the learning accommodation she needed.

People, in general, were nosy and always wanted to know why Kora lived her life the way she did, even if they had just met her. She was always having to defend herself or explain why she was a bit different and what she needed to stay safe and happy. Fitting in was a constant struggle. Kora secretly took extreme precautions not to set anything else off, but it was difficult to be secretive about her aversion to technology. While other kids were beyond addicted to devices like phones and tablets, she was allergic to them.

Kids her age would constantly take selfies, post on social media, plug headphones in their ears, and tune the world out. They exchanged Snapchat photos, scrolled TikTok, watched YouTube, played video games like *Roblox* and *Among Us* for hours, and scrolled. They chose to live in the virtual world and weren't much engaged in the one around them happening in real time under their noses. But Kora could not and did not want to partake in that particular culture, in the same way she refused to eat animals, and it was not a hard decision at all. Her whole heart and body told her to abstain from both meat and technology, so it never felt like avoiding either was a deprivation.

That day in science class, her teacher had no patience for her particular special needs. Mr. Giles instructed everyone to move to the computer lab in the rear of the classroom, log in, and begin the multiple-choice test. He loved pop quizzes because all he had to do was give one that graded itself, and he could kick back all class period and mindlessly scroll on his phone.

Kora sat there, waiting for her paper version, but Mr. Giles forgot to print it out for her that day. He was tired and refused to put in the extra time that her accommodation required.

He whined, "Can't you just take it on the computer like everyone else, just this once? Come on, work with me here, please!" His annoyed eyes were beady. When he pointed his fingers to direct her toward the computer tests, Kora could see the sweat rings from his armpits turning his light blue collared shirt a shade of darker blue.

The last thing Kora wanted to do was make a scene. Mr. Giles had called her out in front of the whole class. She didn't usually have the confidence or voice to speak up for herself. She was a try-not-to-make-waves kind of student. But that day, she had the guts to politely suggest, "I can just take it tomorrow, Mr. Giles, by hand, not on the computer."

Mr. Giles was losing his short temper. "Why are you making my job so tough today, Kora? Sit down at a computer like all the other kids in this day and age, and take the darn test. I let you do the last one with pen and paper, and honestly, that's a lot of extra work for me. Cooperate with me here, please, sweetie." As he said this, the swoop of greased hair that covered his bald spot came loose and flew out in a mesmerizing but horrifying clump.

Kora hated being called out. She would rather blend into the walls like a chameleon, instead of having attention placed on her, especially in front of an entire class. Nobody but Bodi knew of her "thing," and she had kept it on the down low the whole time she was in school. Talking to her directly, in front of the class, about her accommodation felt like a big spotlight on her, and she was expected to sing center stage, which was her biggest nightmare. And then the mean girl, Lizzy, had to chime in and add a comment, in something that was really none of her business, but was playing out in front of everyone. Kora didn't even know how Lizzy knew her name, since they had never talked to each other directly about anything. She always felt that Lizzy gave off an air of condescension, so she avoided interacting with her, going as far as being careful to not even be in close vicinity to her.

All Lizzy said was "Just deal, Kora!" but her snarky tone pushed Kora over the edge, to the fiery side of her aggression. She couldn't control it any longer. As everyone in the classroom started to devolve into a bit of anarchy because the "Mr. Giles versus Kora" paper test dilemma was creating a hiccup for the class, Kora directed her fingers toward Lizzy's back jeans pocket. Lizzy's pocket bulged with her cell phone, tucked away for class, but still on her body. Kora aimed some of the energy from her fingertips at the phone, and added some heat. Kora was vindictive and causing harm for the first time, but nobody saw her do it, because who would expect it?

Lizzy quickly felt her pocket heat up. She pulled her phone out, and it was as hot as a bag of popcorn just out of the microwave. She fumbled it, and dropped it on her desk, pushing on any and all buttons to awaken the screen. Nothing.

Kora knew she broke the phone. But the drama made Lizzy take her attention off Kora and put it all on her phone as she tried to resuscitate it. She would have given it CPR if she could. It was as if her life had just stopped, and she couldn't believe she was suddenly in this position. Kora sank back into her desk, for the first time feeling no remorse and maybe even a bit victorious that she was able to shut the mean girl up. She had used her powers to make Lizzy mind her own stinkin' business.

Satisfied but still pissed, Kora agreed to touch more electronics, just so she could have the moment of "I told you so: Don't mess with me!" as her anger and frustration were about to blow up. Mr. Giles had given her the perfect invitation. She sat down in front of the last free computer in the back of the classroom. Completely aware of what could happen if she made contact with the keyboard, she hovered her fingers over it and felt the heat again.

Kora looked at her reflection on the screen. She pulled her hair back into a ponytail and then took it out, then twisted it into a high bun, and then undid that. She was starting to sweat a bit. Kora was dangerously close to the device she knew would cause a spark but did not know what might happen next after she made contact.

Mr. Giles barked, "Sit here, and take the test, hon. Just do it, for all of us, please."

Kora hated being addressed by that kind of endearment. It made her cringe. It made her feel smaller, inferior, lesser at the hands of a greasy middle-aged man who surely should have had an awakening years ago to realize he was in the wrong line of work. He should have sought happiness by switching it up, but instead, he spent his professional life doing something that did not bring him (or anyone around him) joy.

She had been pushed to feel so angry that she did not even try to practice any of the breathing techniques that Ms. Piper had been teaching her for the last four years—for exactly this kind of moment. Kora was beyond it all. The energy was bubbling up beyond control. Kora began to sense that she was spinning out, unable to get a grip on her cool. Students one by one had completed their tests and were leaving the room for lunch. Mr. Giles was the last to leave, and said, "I will give you through lunch to get it done. Just get it done! OK?"

As she sat alone in front of the screen, suddenly a message popped up. It said, in blinking white type, all caps: "KORA, YOUR POWERS AS ECOQUEEN ARE NEEDED IMMEDIATELY AT COORDINATES N 46°32'38", W 48°29'53". PLEASE PRESS CONTROL + E + Q NOW. TRUST ME! —RÍO."

CHAPTER 12

RÍO CALLING

CALIFORNIA

As she continued to stare at the screen in confusion, a video chat opened.

"Kora, I am Río." A dark-haired teenage boy about her age was talking to her through the computer screen, looking right at her with eyes that seemed strangely familiar—emerald green. Even though it was screen-to-screen communication, their connection felt very real. It was not as shocking as maybe it should have been that this stranger on the computer called her by name, because it felt like she might have known him from somewhere before.

He smiled giddily while talking to her. In his excitement, he started to stutter, but then he got it under control. Kora waited as he took a breath.

"I am Río! I am Río!" he kept saying. His communication skills seemed a bit off, a little too persistent. He repeated this sentence like she would know what he was talking about when he finally shared his name. But Kora didn't know what to say. Careful not to touch anything on the keyboard, she spoke to this interesting new friend.

"Río . . . like *river* in Spanish?" she replied for some reason. It was all she could think of at first. Then her questions came rapid-fire: "Who are you? Where are you? Why are you talking to me? How do you know me?" This boy had just popped into her life.

"I am your brother." No dancing around the subject for Río. Kora sensed that Río said what he needed to say with no fluff. That was the way he ticked. His smile spread proudly from ear to ear, and he stared right at Kora, on the other side of the screen, even though they were worlds away.

She was completely lost.

"What? How? I don't have a brother. I mean, I'm adopted, so I guess anything is possible. But what makes you think we're siblings?"

"We were born in Ecuador, you and me, on the same day. We are twins . . . same mom and dad. Same womb. We were womb mates." He cracked himself up. "Joke, get it?"

Río had an interesting accent, Kora noticed—not quite British. Maybe South African? From New Zealand? This was all so weird.

Kora knew that her life had started in Ecuador. How many other people knew that about her? She focused on the stature of the boy on the screen, who appeared to be about the same height and build as her. She had never considered that she might have a twin brother, and she was hesitant to believe a video-chatting stranger. However, she was also intrigued. "Tell me something else that only you would know about me, if you really are my brother."

"After we were born in Ecuador, our mom was going to take us to China where she was working on her rainforest project. You caught a cold before our flight to Beijing, so you stayed behind in the jungle where our dad is from with his mother, Abuela Rosa. She was going to bring you to us when you were well, but you were taken. You got lost from us . . . until now."

Kora had never heard anything like this about her history. She wasn't sure if she should believe this guy. Hacking was a thing, and you couldn't just trust anyone you met online, that much she knew. First, she needed to wrap her mind around the fact that maybe she had a brother. But then to believe she had a twin brother? A womb mate? Technically, it was possible. . . . What motivation could he possibly have to lie to her about all this?

"We were separated. You got adopted. I am here in Australia with Mum and Dad."

"What?" Now, this was too much to process at one time. "Prove to me we are related."

"That's easy, and I knew you would ask, so I obtained a sample of your DNA, to do a sibling test. It is an old technology that counts short tandem repeats on a small set of autosomal markers that reflect genetic contributions of both parents. The last time you ate at Wildflower with your friend Bodi, I had an operative send a sample of your spit removed from your water glass, and I ran the analysis. Look, we are the same!" He put his head down and typed vigorously on his keyboard like a professional pianist, with the same energy of creating some kind of masterpiece with his fingers alone. The screen changed to a circular graph with an almost identical comparison of the double helix DNA markers.

"Yours—mine. Mum also says we have matching bracelets." He held up his left wrist to show off a band with a small section of bright red, yellow, and green beadwork. "When we were tiny babies, Abuela Rosa made us matching necklaces. But babies grow. So what fit our necks then fits our wrists now. Twin bracelets. For twins."

All she could do was stare, mouth open, at this person on the screen and try to wrap her mind around what she was hearing. She wanted to know more.

"We have been watching you for the last several years with satellite video to make sure it was you. And to keep an eye on you over there. I am just glad we found you! I could have found you much sooner if you interacted with computers more."

"Yeah, I kind of . . . have a thing," she replied, not sure how much she wanted to reveal.

"I know you do! It is because you are from our family. Mum, Dad, me, you. I have a thing, too."

This piqued her interest. "So, what's your thing?"

"I have figured out how to help you teletransport to get to hot spots that need you and your superpowers the most. It is easy. I can get inside the computers. I write algorithms that change the way people do things." Río was proud of what others sometimes judged him for.

"Wait, go back—superpowers??"

"I wanted you to know that it is time to help us fight climate change. We have been working hard here on developing the teletransportation, identifying your powers, finding you, prioritizing the hot spots, and working on the seeds. We need you. Can you be on our team? The world needs someone with superpowers right now to fight global warming.

Nothing else is working, and we are losing. You have the power to help.
We know you can do it. You have what it takes. We have a plan, but we
need you to go, act, help the people being affected by climate change.
The world needs a climate superhero!"

They locked eyes. Kora understood him and the plight of the world,
even if she still didn't understand how she could use her powers in this
fight.

"I will help," Río said, "but you need to use your electrokinesis: your
psychic power to manipulate energies. Getting the world to stop using
fossil fuels is taking way too long. Time is running out. Temperatures
around the earth are rising, throwing everything off balance. Scientists
say that we have only three more years to reduce global temperatures
by three degrees Celsius. We need change now, and nobody is taking
charge. *You* can! You have as much energy as the sun. Figure out what
to do with that, EcoQueen."

"EcoQueen! Huh, I think I like that!" Río had convinced Kora. "OK,
OK! Count me in."

Río rubbed his hands together. "Ready, EcoQueen?"

"Ahhh, not really . . . What do I have to do?"

"You are supposed to say, 'I was born ready!' Then press the key
combination: Control, E for Eco, and Q for Queen," Río said.

"OK . . . 'I was born ready?'" Kora's fingers hovered over the keyboard. For the first time, she willingly laid her fingertips on computer
keys: Control, *E*, and *Q*. As predicted, a red spark jumped up from her
hands, and fire and smoke ensued.

Just as the alarms started going off in the school, she was headed
somewhere else.

CHAPTER 13

WELCOME, ECOQUEEN

ARCTIC OCEAN

Kora was jolted as electrical magnetism grabbed at her with extreme force and pulled her, headfirst, into the computer. She splashed through the LCD screen in a dive, right through the plane that acted as the division between reality and the virtual world, and she was in. Having no control over the matter, she entered the world of pixel travel. Kora flew through the realm where text and emails, web pages, photo transmission, and data sharing occurred. It was chaotic and disorienting as she moved quickly through time and space. The temperature was soaring. As quickly as emails flew from one computer to another, Kora did, too, holding on for dear life to the fiber-optic cables and data streams that were zip-lining her to a foreign location on the ocean floor.

Somehow she was delivered to the coordinates from the message, landing her smack at the bottom of the Arctic Ocean, three hundred feet below the surface of the water and miles off the closest shore.

Kora had no oxygen tank, but somehow she could breathe underwater. Somehow, she suddenly felt she had superhuman powers. She was in a special full-body suit—tight, blue, and green, with a cape that drifted gently in the water behind her—and some high-tech features to keep her warm, breathing, and safe. Where did this suit come from?

Was she actually EcoQueen, a superhero with a suit, powers, and everything?

At first notice, the seawater around her was not right. Blotting out all color was a viscous, ink-like substance gushing from a joint where an oil pipe had dislocated from the source. Kora tried to make sense of the scene she had been transported to. The sudden displacement didn't even have time to settle in, when nearby, a shocked whale sent out a high-pitched cry that spoke for all the living creatures in that sea. Kora clearly understood it to mean *Help! Please do something!*

The whale was well aware that his whole ocean community was under siege. Oil was spilling into the open waters, oil that for millions of years sat undisturbed underground, until recently. Something had gone drastically wrong. *Leaking* would be too tame a word to describe the rate at which the oil erupted from the ocean floor; it was more like volcanic-eruption speed. The pipe and reinforced concrete cylinders had become dislodged from their airtight position and no longer connected the massive drill pipes to the enormous oil rig, which had just been put online. At a rate of about one thousand gallons a minute, the leak gushed into the water like blood from a head wound. Thick black crude oil poured out into the Arctic seawaters and swirled before fully mixing and taking over as if the black oil was at war with the colors of the rainbow in the ocean.

Further intel came in from Kora's suit. "EcoQueen, it's Río. Use your powers now! It is time. Any marine life that is near this oil spill will be smothered. You only have minutes before this oil destroys the whole ecosystem."

In the confusion around her, his determined voice grounded her. For a moment she imagined him in his headquarters (his bedroom in a different hemisphere). Río had probably already over-researched the climate disaster. He must have a plan, but she had so many questions: "Río, where am I? How can I breathe underwater? Why am I here?"

Río started to stutter, but then slowed down. His answer refocused her on the mission. "You are on the Jeanne d'Arc Basin off Newfoundland in the Arctic at the brand-new $14 billion Hebron Field, currently pumping 180,000 barrels of oil a day, which helps feed the United States' twenty-million-barrels-a-day oil addiction. It took years to build and one iceberg to destroy it. You have to stop the flow. Use your superpowers."

She sensed that this was not the time to debate or wait for an answer to her other questions. Kora became EcoQueen in that instant and trusted that all she needed to do was unleash the potential energy she had been trying to contain until now. It was like she was given the OK to let it rip.

The water was too cold, and ordinary human rescue or repair efforts would be difficult. It wasn't very different from the historic Deepwater Horizon oil spill in April 2010 in the Gulf of Mexico, which was considered the biggest oil spill in the petroleum industry's history. That had resulted in an oil spill that continued for over three months in severity and was still leaking.

Río, as if reading her mind, shared some stats. "The Deepwater Horizon oil spill killed 82,000 birds, 25,900 marine mammals, 6,000 sea turtles, and tens of thousands of fish. This Arctic catastrophe is about to cause even more destruction, so, EcoQueen, you need to do something about it quickly!"

She panicked for one hot second and then realized that she had to pull it together and do something, fast! With her eyes closed and the palms of her hands raised in front of her as if she were ready to stop a train, she attempted to gather the electricity within her. She entered into a moment where she could not see or hear or feel any distractions around her. Hearkening back to the times on the beach training with Ms. Piper, she hoped she could muster the same powers she had when throwing energy around with her teacher. She closed her eyes and reenacted the time she was able to roll the boulder five times her height.

Río radioed into the speakers in her hood: "Use the energy of your emotions and channel it into making the change you want to see in your world." He had the gift, sometimes the curse, of being able to tune into others' emotions, and seeing and hearing them loud and clear. Often, he would mistake others' feelings as his own. But he knew she had to do something, quickly, and since she was there and he was not, he had to give her words of encouragement to act.

The situation was bizarre, but at the same time, Kora knew that she was made for this. Kora, now channeling EcoQueen, felt her hands shaking and heating up like the high voltage was revving up to release out of her palms, and she let it burst. The electricity that came shooting from her palms didn't make any impact because she hadn't yet focused it on the problem area. She had power, but it wasn't going in the right direction.

She pumped the energy by raising and lowering her hands like she did to control the waves on the beach. Now, in the face of a crisis, she created turbulence in the deep waters that built up a tsunami-like wall of water.

Oh no, too much! Not what I wanted.

She dropped her hands. She had to figure out a way to deal with the wound on the ocean floor oozing the black blood of crude oil.

Ok, I got this, I got this. She was big on positive self-talk. With intense concentration, she connected the energy from her hands with the mangled shards of metal that littered the ocean floor from the destroyed rig. Acting like a magnet, EcoQueen drew the metals close to her. As she turned up the heat, she transformed the scrap metal into its molten form. She stretched this new material as effortlessly as making finger taffy, swirling it together in front of her body to form a barrier like a cap she could place over the broken ocean floor. Little did she know the science of the chemical reaction she had created in front of her, but intuitively she had synthesized a new material, creating ridiculously strong molecules. The metal was two hundred times stronger than steel and was strong enough to stop the rush of oil.

Through the speakers in her superhero suit, she heard a voice say, "Yes, good job, EcoQueen! Mildred S. Dresselhaus is one of my heroes. She is the queen of carbon science! She carried out a series of experiments that led to the fundamental understanding of the electronic structure of semimetals, which you are using now. Well done."

EcoQueen tossed the undersea material like pizza dough and placed it over the gaping hole—a very heavy Band-Aid. With her bare hands, she sealed around the perimeter of the hole using more heat and energy. Kora contained the oil beneath the ground, putting it gently back to bed like a baby under its covers. The reparative surgery she performed on the earth had already begun to heal. Most importantly, she stopped the bleeding of oil and averted a catastrophic disaster.

But while she was at it, she melted the rest of the oil rig so it could not be repaired or ever be operational again. This action made her grin. It was inconceivable how many marine animals she had saved. Because of EcoQueen's heroism, it was a far better outcome than the world's worst oil spills before. This catastrophe became a nonevent. Mission accomplished.

"Grab onto the communications cable again!" Río prompted.

In that one minute, which felt like an eternity, she traveled through the fiber-optic cable, through the computer, and popped out this time into a smoked-out classroom, the computer screen not yet melted. Kora was back to where she was sitting when she touched the computer, the spot from which she started the journey. Fire blazed from the monitor. Smoke alarms pierced her eardrums.

The fire drill that students practiced every year at school since kindergarten was being carried out for real, but most of her fellow students didn't realize the severity of the danger. Before the indoor sprinkler systems were triggered, Kora had the presence of mind to grab a nearby fire extinguisher to blast the computer. Even though the flames were out, the air quality was still horrible.

Kora ran to the exit door and out of the school. Her hair was still wet from her underwater mission in the Arctic Ocean. She looked down at herself. She was back in her hoodie and yoga pants with flip-flops. She looked normal enough as she ran outside to where the other students were congregated and being counted. Many of the kids were experiencing PTSD, as it had been only a few weeks since the wildfire ripped through their hometown, sparing their school, the last safe haven for many. To these teenagers, lately, it felt like it was some new catastrophe every week concerning climate change. The fire trucks were pulling up.

Kora grabbed Bodi's arm in line, as four more fire trucks arrived and Mr. Giles called out, "Kora Greenway?"

"Here!" she responded, but she felt a million miles away.

She looked like she had returned from battle. Her eyes were wide and her expression ghostly as she tried to adapt to this new situation she was thrown into just as fast as the other one, under the ocean. At least she was standing beside her best friend, Bodi.

"Oh my god, Kora, what kept you? I was freaking out! Are you OK?"

Kora could barely formulate words. "I'm OK."

"I seriously was about to run back inside a possibly burning building to look for you. You scared the crap out of me when I couldn't find you out here. Where were you?" Bodi gave her a big hug. He turned his backpack around to the front and unzipped the small pocket so he could take a hit off his inhaler. He couldn't tell if his heart was racing from asthma or just adrenaline. Nonetheless, he reached for something to calm him.

"I'm not quite sure what I was doing. I went somewhere else," Kora confided.

"I'm glad you're here and safe now. I was really worried." He gave her another big hug.

What had happened to her? Where did she go? When and how could she talk to Río again to get some answers?

CHAPTER 14

RECKONING WITH ECOQUEEN

CALIFORNIA

The electrical surge at the school was Kora's doing, she knew for sure, but she also knew not to say a thing. If the school knew she had started the fire, they would take disciplinary action. The building was closed down indefinitely as the school district worked on the terminal electrical problems throughout the building. You couldn't run a school without lights, electricity, internet, lunches. In a scramble from the unprecedented school closure, the administration sent all the students home to learn online until the building could be brought back to functionality. Nobody knew how long until the problem was resolved. Kora wasn't ready to take all that blame.

Kora and Bodi usually went to the beach together almost every day after school, so they decided to follow their routine, despite the day being so far from the norm. Bodi jumped in the cold surf to clear his head, as he often did. Something about a cold water plunge always set him right, jolted him into the present moment, forced him to breathe. Getting a little pounded by the energy of the breaking waves also physically set him straight. He had a love affair with the ocean and all the cleansing it offered.

While Bodi bodysurfed in the shore-break waves, Kora practiced a few rounds of her chi gung on the sand, thinking about the rescue she had made on the seafloor of the Arctic Ocean using this power in her hands. It was clear that this was a gift that she had to learn how to use for the greater good. The oil-spill mission replayed over and over again in her head as she continued to question if it was real or just a dream. Privately she tormented herself, but she knew it must have happened because she could vividly recall the feeling, the wet coldness, the power radiating, the conflict resolved, and the rush of adrenaline from the epic save of that entire ecosystem. It was huge.

She couldn't stop thinking about the boy, Río, who had talked her through it all and seemed to be looking out for her. She bathed in that feeling of someone new taking care of her, on her team—another person besides Bodi who had her back. The boy who claimed he was her twin. It was so much to process on her own, she had to tell someone about it, but she knew she would sound delusional.

Kora liked that Bodi was a loyal friend, and he liked that Kora was low maintenance, down to earth, and easy to talk to. Their friendship was effortless, supportive, and fun, as friendships should be. They had both been through so many different friend scenarios that became lame in the end. They were psyched to finally find each other and not worry about the pressures of fitting in anymore. It is a gift to have a friend who you can be yourself around, where things are natural and easy.

Bodi's resting expression was a fresh braces-fixed smile that was contagious. He always seemed content and was easy to be around; Bodi didn't get tied up in drama or high school social distraction. Kora and Bodi didn't care much for the big gatherings, so they stayed peripheral, but together. Bodi's looks made lots of girls get silly and weird and overly flirty around him, which made him shy. He preferred authenticity over trying to impress. He was a self-proclaimed introvert, most content when he got to spend time by himself, happiest when surfing out in the ocean alone, making fresh food at home, riding his bike, or playing his guitar. He loved hanging out with Kora.

Kora was one of the only people Bodi knew who was all there, not distracted. She was mentally and emotionally available whenever they hung out, mostly because she was not on the phone, checking it instead of checking in with the person right in front of her. The rest of their classmates had fallen victim to the nervous habit of using their phone as a life preserver—holding them up, pulling them in—when the world around them felt uncomfortable. Kora disliked phones and computers so much that Bodi would step in as Kora's secretary in the few but mandatory times she had to communicate through devices. He didn't mind, and Kora seemed to really appreciate it.

When Bodi got out of the water, Kora wrapped him in the oversize beach towel, opening it wide so he could back up into it. Blythe used to call this "Mommy Towel You!" an offering of warmth and embrace when Kora would get out of a bath or pool. Kora had loved it, so to this day she spontaneously offered the love up to her friend whenever he got out of the frigid water.

He turned around and smiled his perfect smile at her, the one that said without saying, *Thanks, I am grateful for you!*

That trusting, loving smile propelled Kora to finally share what she could no longer keep to herself. Her mom wasn't there for her to confide in, but Bodi could be.

"Bodi, I have to tell you something. When everyone else in class was headed for a break after that test and the fire alarm sounded, I was off making a rescue."

"What kind of rescue? And off where?" Bodi responded while shaking the towel through his sandy curls.

"Well, pretty much, I guess I saved the earth from the devastating effects of climate change and massive pollution." What a relief it was to finally get it off her chest and share with someone, to validate it wasn't something she'd made up in her head.

"Well, thank goodness. Someone has to do something about the mess we're in!" Bodi always knew Kora went the extra mile to do what was right in the name of the environment, secretly turning down the water heater in her house to conserve energy and picking through the garbage to sort out cans and glass that ended up in the wrong bin because of someone else's laziness. She was also the best thrifter he knew, taking reusing and recycling to the ultimate with her clothing choices. She avoided new clothing and supporting the fast-fashion industry, which she felt was part of the problem. Bodi loved the patchwork comfy pants she made for him where she sewed together two pant legs from two different sweatpants and then funked them out with a lightning-bolt ribbon stripe down the legs. She was always attempting something for the betterment of the environment. So, Bodi was not surprised, but he still did not quite understand the massiveness of the mission she alluded to. "How did you save the world today? Did you go get that compost bin you told me about for the cafeteria?"

"No, Bodi. What I mean is, I did something huge and kind of superhuman. I still don't really understand how it happened. This guy who calls himself Río popped up on my computer. He says he is my brother. And somehow he sent me into the ocean . . . through the internet or something."

"*What?*"

"I know, it sounds weird. Bodi, it IS weird! I was basically teletransported and delivered to a . . . climate emergency . . . at the bottom of the ocean in the Arctic! To the scene of a devastating oil spill." As she told the story, she paused, realizing that while she said the words aloud, it didn't even sound real to her. "There was oil spilling out of the ocean floor in a black pillar that I repaired with my own two hands and some electrical powers that came out of my fingertips." She knew that it probably wouldn't make much sense to anyone. It sounded like crazy sci-fi.

"Wait, what? Are you sure you are OK? When my dad left, for a while, nothing seemed real. It was like I was just living in a dream. . . . Do you think you might be dealing with something like that now? Maybe all you are going through with your mom, and then the smoke today . . . ?"

"You know my thing with devices? How I can't even touch computers? I was pissed at Lizzy for making me embarrassed and mad at Giles for forcing me to do a test on the computer, but then I got drawn in by this message, from this Río guy, that showed up on the screen. I must have made the spark that started the school fire, but then I wasn't even there anymore. I was at the scene of what could have been complete devastation, and I fixed it. I got there and used superpowers, the ones I have been trying to tame with the martial arts. Well, I went all out. You have to believe me. Please, I'm not hallucinating. Remember, my hair was all wet?" she said.

Bodi immediately got on board, even if he didn't seem to understand it all. To be fair, Kora didn't really understand it herself. He said, "Well, someone had to do something to save the environment. . . . The earth needs a superhero right now because shit is getting real! We all need to do what we can to help."

"Thanks, Bodi. I'll keep you posted, OK? I'm feeling kind of wiped out after all this excitement, but I think I'd better check in with Ms. Piper to see if she can explain what's going on with me. And maybe my dad, too—now that I've heard from someone who says he's my birth family."

Bodi gave Kora a salty, encouraging hug. "OK, Kora. Stay strong. If anyone can help us get out of this climate crisis, I have no doubt it's you! And good luck with your dad."

She couldn't quite sense if Bodi completely understood the gravity of her actions. But at least she told him, and he heard it, and he didn't freak out.

"Want to meet here tomorrow?" he asked. "We have nothing to do but hang until they figure out how to have school without a school to go to. My mom texted that she's been at an emergency parent-teacher meeting at the community center, but they don't have anything ready for us yet."

"Sure," she said. "That sounds like a plan. I'll meet you here after breakfast." She waved to Bodi as he hopped on his bike to ride home and cook dinner for his mom before she got home from the school meeting.

Kora's world had been turned upside down. She was still trying to make sense of Río, her mission, her school, her powers—all the while trying to process the crash course of how to exist in a world without a mom. Thank goodness Bodi seemed to be taking it all in stride.

And then she realized it was a training day with Ms. Piper. Kora was so relieved to see her beloved teacher walking down the beach, coming toward her in her loose-fitting rolled-up black comfy karate pants. Just the person she needed to fall apart with at that moment . . .

Ms. Piper could tell that Kora needed help. Even more than Kora herself, she could sense when Kora was more in her head than her body.

Now, as she saw her teacher and mentor, Kora finally had her mental breakdown in order to have a breakthrough. The dam broke, her tears flowed, and Ms. Piper, who was waiting for this to happen, just held her, so Kora could get all the fear, sadness, confusion, frustration, and emotion out in the one good cry she had been holding on to for far too long.

"What am I supposed to do?" Kora finally said aloud. It was the existential moment that had her taking a deep dive into how she wanted or needed to proceed after all the events that had set her on a particular path.

Ms. Piper, a woman who mostly showed herself to the world by her actions, doing and being, rather than her words, put her hands on Kora's shoulders and looked right into her green eyes, which were filled with tears and a whole lot of hurt and confusion.

Ms. Piper said, "Do what your heart knows is right. You have gifts. You know what they are. Step fully into yourself and tap into what you can offer the world. I know you know why you were put on this earth and what you can offer to the world right now!"

Kora felt like she was receiving the permission she needed, as if Ms. Piper hit the Go button on her sternum. Her heart felt full, her feet grounded in the warmth of the sand, and her intentions were clear, for the first time in her life. She breathed in.

Ms. Piper communicated the rest of what she had to impart to Kora without a single word. They both faced the waves side by side. They began their form of synchronized motion to start manipulating energy. When Kora felt the juices flowing, and locked into the skill and expression that came so naturally to her, it was as if something clicked into place, and the direction was clear. She knew what she needed to use her superpowers for. She felt able to embrace her true calling to become EcoQueen.

"My heart feels like it is shattered into a million pieces for my mom, I can't even describe the pain, and it seems to be fueling this energy I've been trying to curb with you. Now it just wants to come out, and fight, do something. If I can save another kid from this grief, from losing a parent to climate change, then absolutely, I want to do what I can."

That night, after her school's meltdown and the epiphany with Ms. Piper, Kora rode her bike back home to the hotel room where she was living with her dad. She was feeling oddly at peace. She felt ready to ask him about whether he'd ever heard anything about her having a twin, or if she'd been wearing a beaded necklace when they picked her up from the orphanage.

Her dad was watching the news, so he barely even noticed that she had come in. He had taken off his suit jacket and tie, and had his white undershirt still on with a belt and slacks, as if he'd dropped everything for the TV.

The meticulously done-up anchorwoman, in her blue dress and perfectly highlighted hair, looked into the camera lens and reported, "Today, the world's largest iceberg almost collided with the world's largest oil rig. A seventeen-mile crack in the Petermann Glacier near Newfoundland finally calved due to rising temperatures and began to drift along the Labrador Current. It drifted across the barren Arctic Ocean like an unmanned ship the size of an unanchored small island. But thanks to six fighter jets, flanked by eight military drones, the American air force saved the day by dropping low-level nuclear bombs on the rogue iceberg, averting a collision with the $14 billion Hebron oil rig."

Duncan, already informed of this close call, let out a big breath after his very stressful day. "And thank the Lord the thing is still pumping! I cannot handle an Ecuador-like fiasco with a project going under again!" he said out loud to himself.

Kora watched the news' commentary in disbelief and thought, *That is not what I experienced today!* But she was psyched to know that she averted a complete disaster. She definitely did not want or need any credit, either as Kora or as EcoQueen. She did appreciate the satisfaction of knowing that she had saved that whale and countless other creatures, and her powers had protected an entire biome. Not bad for a Tuesday.

Duncan finally looked up to acknowledge Kora. "Oh, what time is it? You're home! How was school?"

"Oh, it was evacuated today! Almost burned down. Will be closed for a while."

Characteristically, Kora's dad was late to the game in all things school related. He had been focused again on his own world that was crashing down at work, so now his family life continued to fall around him, too. He recognized that he had missed another big situation where he should have been available for his daughter but hadn't been.

Overwhelmed, he scratched his head as they both pondered how they could make things better.

CHAPTER 15

FINDING A MISSION

CALIFORNIA

Since the electrical fry at the high school, students weren't able to return until the administration got the building up and running again. Usually, it takes a few hours or maybe a few days to restore electricity after an emergency, but the school power loss caused extensive damage, so it was taking much longer to rewire the building. In its eighty-seven years, during the scheduled school year, Tram High School had never been shut down to students for more than a day. But without electricity, lights, Wi-Fi, ventilation, or a cafeteria, it couldn't serve the community. For the kids who had always hoped for some doomsday excuse to not have to go back to school, it was a dream come true. But once they could not go back to the place where they spent their days, or keep any of their routines, it was quite disorienting. It was especially difficult for those who did not have a support system or the inner discipline and motivation to finish their schoolwork on their own time. Some kids had the additional hurdle of a lack of access to (or in Kora's case, an inability to touch) technology.

The teachers taught from their homes, where you could get a glimpse of their living room or kitchen. Students learned from home, never having to get out of their pajamas, or their bed, for that matter. Everyone stayed home and attempted to jump into a remote learning experience, while crews worked around the clock trying to get the school back up and running. Some students dropped off the radar completely, unaccountable ever since the electrical surge. Others were forced to adapt abruptly to their new reality. If nothing else, these high schoolers were learning the lesson of how life can change course overnight.

Luckily, Kora and Bodi were two students who liked learning and valued their access to education. Although remote online learning might have been the end of Kora's high school career due to her little issue with computers, Bodi stepped up as her IT guy. Kora still had to steer clear of the devices, even though her electricity control was getting pretty high level from the work she had been doing with Ms. Piper. So, Bodi helped her out in that department.

Every weekday, Kora went over to Bodi's trailer and let him navigate the video calls, and they attended virtual classes together. She had mostly the same classes as Bodi, but at the start of the school year, some of them were at different periods. Luckily, in the figure-it-out-as-you-go mentality, now that learning was all remote, their teachers were flexible enough to let Bodi and Kora switch to the same schedule. The instructors were just grateful to have Kora still learning and not throwing another wrench in their syllabi with her special accommodations. It didn't seem so important to be strict about who was supposed to be watching what class when.

Bodi set his laptop to play on his family's TV. They turned the screen around and put it on the breakfast table, so they could sit outside in the sun and still see it. Outdoor learning wasn't so bad. Learning from a hammock was quite the improvement from a stuffy classroom under fluorescent lights with no breeze and the distinct aroma of gym floor and cafeteria meatloaf. Kora actually preferred their new setup to in-school classes, as long as Bodi could drive the tech for them.

Bodi's deck was an instant school as long as they had internet service. This sunny morning, they were in virtual Spanish class, learning about the historic Hurricane Maria that had ravaged Puerto Rico. Since one of the few things Kora knew about her birth life was that she was adopted from Ecuador, she identified as Latina, and that motivated her to learn Spanish as her second language. She knew the language was in her brain somewhere from her first year of life, so she figured she just had to help get it out.

She was dedicated to perfecting her Spanish because she had the fantasy that if she met her biological parents someday, she would want to be able to communicate with them, not just stare in amazement. She was taking AP Spanish, the highest-level Spanish she could take at her high school, and had a pretty good accent, yet she could understand better than she could speak. Bodi had also been pushing himself pretty hard so someday he might be comfortable visiting his dad and his new family in Costa Rica. Their teacher, Señora Flora, had posted a short article in Spanish. The assignment was to read the article and answer reading-comprehension questions.

Kora offered, "I'll read it out loud." She read quite fluently, in an accent that was more Mexican than Castilian. Bodi and Kora had a good tag team thing going on, and complemented each other academically as well as socially. Kora often recited a quote her mom would often say, "Two heads together solving a problem is always better than one!"

Bodi and Kora got the gist of the article. But they struggled some trying to absorb the facts about the enormity of the destruction to infrastructure, the humanitarian crisis, and the longest disruption in electricity service in the history of the US, all caused by one hurricane. They were shocked by the horrific number of deaths, both during the storm and in the days and weeks that followed. What they really couldn't believe was that it seemed like the world hadn't learned much of a lesson from it all.

"So, 4,727 people died, and our government still pulled the country out of the Paris Agreement?" Kora felt sick about the shortsightedness of leadership that would leave its people so vulnerable after such a devastating event. Backing out of a global response to climate change seemed almost like criminal negligence.

Bodi typed up their assignments as they talked it over. As Bodi responded to the last question on the homework, Río suddenly appeared on his computer screen.

"Kora, it is fortuitous that you are studying about a hurricane of biblical proportions, as there is another one right now in the Caribbean, and people there need your help."

Bodi peered closely at this guy on the screen who looked just like the boy from the monitor in environmental science class that Kora had described to him after her first mission.

Kora looked at Bodi's surprised face and nodded. "Yup, Bodi, this is Río, the guy I told you about who has started popping up in my life for some reason."

Río, not attuned to social norms and never one to give any attention to social cues, proceeded to drop an information download on Kora: "The National Weather Service is reporting this hurricane, called Donny, is pummeling the Caribbean. Hurricane Donny is currently a category 5, which is still rapidly intensifying on the leeward side of the islands while moving over warmer water and into a more moist atmosphere with maximum sustained winds of 185 miles per hour. Even after making landfall, it is that strong. This may be the strongest hurricane ever observed in the Atlantic Ocean, breaking the records of Irma and Maria. Resources are going to be extremely strained in the aftermath of this." He said very seriously, "You need to go right now!"

"Right now? I have homework. . . ."

"This is epically more important than homework. The island needs you. The storm has passed, after pounding the island for hours, but the damage is widespread. More homes and lives will be lost. They are going to need a lot of assistance right away. No other emergency services can get in with the storm still in the area. I can get you there for some relief efforts right now. Just touch the computer."

"I feel like I just got back from the last crazy mission, and I'm still processing it all. Can't I have a few days to recover?"

"EcoQueen, these climate events seem to be coming one after another. I wish there was some lull in between, but right now, with the state of the environment, they are stacking up, and you are one of the only people I know with powers who can help. Because you can save these lives, you have to go."

"Kora, if they need you and if you can help, go for it!" Bodi chimed in.

"Alright, alright—I'm convinced. What do I have to do next, Río? Send me there, I'll do it."

CHAPTER 16

THE HURRICANE'S AFTERMATH

PUERTO RICO

She arrived in a war zone caused by nature, not a human villain, so it was hard to place blame. The "act of God" some called it, known as a hurricane, hit down on the island with such force, the islanders were without electricity, drinking water, food, or medicine. Hurricane Donny made a direct hit over the island, and it destroyed everything in its path.

EcoQueen scanned the scene and noticed that the palm trees looked more like flagpoles, since every leaf had been blown off them and most were on the ground. Before her, a world was upside down. Splintered boats lay on their sides with no water beneath them anymore; yachts and fishing boats were thrown onto the shore. It looked like anything that was not bolted down took flight during the hurricane winds, and anything that was supposed to be dry was now saturated from the hurricane rains. A soup of mess squelched beneath her feet, and the stench of things moist for too long was just beginning.

EcoQueen's high-tech suit regulated her body temperature to adapt to the suffocating island heat and humidity, keeping her relatively cool despite the tropical sun. EcoQueen, along with all the survivors, started a list of what she once took for granted, like shade, air-conditioning, the ability to call her family, refrigeration to keep food from spoiling, and a roof. Almost every house had at least a major section of the roof ripped off, making every household even more vulnerable and exposed to the elements.

EcoQueen's stout black leather boots, with the extra-thick special soles, crunched the shards of glass sprinkled all over the ground, carnage from blown-out windows. She carefully stepped over piles of metal shards and splintered wood, and the extra balancers built into her boots helped her walk confidently over the road of destruction. Río, who was standing by at mission control many time zones away, was closely following her movement via the device sewn into the special nanothreads used to construct her suit, which covered her body in wearable technology like a living, moving computer center.

The entire island of Puerto Rico was without electricity again. The hurricane had snapped all the power lines. Little did anyone know that it would be months before power would be restored. It was PTSD, and the islanders couldn't believe they were living through another Maria. However, nothing had really changed since the last megahurricane that hit their island, and they felt like a hurricane target.

EcoQueen saw a mom with a baby on her hip, a toddler who had just started walking clinging to her leg, a seven-year-old trying so hard to keep it together, and a fourteen-year-old who was assuming the responsibilities of a mom, since her adult in charge was in such utter shock that she was mentally paralyzed from the trauma. Four kids, no house, no energy, no water, no food. After a night of horror, torrential rain, and frightening winds, they were in survival mode. The family stood in front of the rubble that had once been their home. The place where the mom had confidently fed, protected, sheltered, bathed, and raised her children existed no longer.

EcoQueen walked over to the family gathered in disbelief. Sometimes it took days or weeks to finally accept the reality of sudden devastation. EcoQueen could see the denial, and that the mom was in a state of shock, while the daughters were overblown with emotion and tears. Their refrigerator was in their front lawn, their patio furniture blew over to their neighbors' yards, full walls were missing from their house. The windows were shattered even though plywood reinforcement had been installed before the storm. Obviously the screws were not long enough, or tight enough, or the wood wasn't strong enough, as Hurricane Donny had ripped siding right from the house. Their mattresses were waterlogged and disgusting, and if anything from the house was miraculously not tossed into the yard, it sat in waist-high mud and stagnant water.

The oldest daughter seemed to grow up into the head of the family overnight. Her name was Lola. She looked older than her age, her hips and chest developed like a grown woman, the only thing that gave her youth away was the patch of pimples on her forehead. She was only in eighth grade. She had heard that her school was destroyed in the hurricane, so was she really in the eighth grade anymore if there was no school to go back to? All she had left to her name were the clothes on her back—a tasseled shirt and the flowy striped cotton pants she was wearing when the hurricane hit. She had lost a sandal somewhere between running from her falling-apart house to a neighbor's to avoid the floodwaters, but she found a stray flip-flop that was floating and slipped it on her shoeless foot. And this was the second time this family had survived a life-threatening hurricane like this.

The family was not even fazed that a stranger in a cape was approaching them. All EcoQueen had to say was, "Are you guys OK?" That was finally the release Lola needed to let it all out and recount what had happened to her. Like witnessing a car accident, sometimes you have to confer with someone else to validate what you actually saw. EcoQueen's invitation to share allowed Lola to speak of her experience and process for the first time what she had lived through.

"The wind was screaming. In the middle of the night, it was pure darkness so you couldn't see what was flying around outside. And then it ripped the roof right off our house like peeling open a can! Our family ran up to our neighbor's, holding on to each other to not let anyone drift away. The water was up to my waist. We pounded on their door, yelling. They let us in, but a whole bunch of water came in with us. We were all upstairs in the bedroom that only had one window, and we prayed it would just stop, but the slapping of the shutters and cracking of the wind made me jump with every smack. It was chaos outside—and in my head.

"I finally went outside this morning, after no sleep and still no food. Our neighborhood isn't the place I grew up anymore. My street is a hazard, not a place to play. It's like a tree and garbage graveyard. You can't walk down the sidewalks unless you're a spider climbing up and over the piles. The floodwaters have nowhere to go. Nothing is the same anymore."

Lola started to cry again, reliving the nightmare. Within a few hours of the passing of the storm, nature was calm and tranquil, even if Lola, her family, and her neighbors still felt their own violent trauma.

She stared at the mismatched shoes on her feet. "My grandparents, my cousins, my aunts, my best friend, I haven't heard from any of them. The phones and internet are down, so I have no idea of who in my family survived this. I don't know if they made it through like we did. We can't connect to see, since all power is down." Lola started to choke up again, as the reality that she was homeless sank into another level. For the first time in her life, Lola wondered where she would find her food, water, and shelter for that night.

EcoQueen walked with her.

"I got you, girl. There is a little something I can do that might help," EcoQueen said. "The sun is beating down hard right here. I have an idea."

EcoQueen stepped away over uneven ground covered in once-important possessions that were drenched, crushed, and splintered. The smell of the tropical air mixed with rotting trash started to surface as a time indicator of how much longer this detritus could lie around before it was dealt with.

EcoQueen found some open space on a concrete foundation where a house had once been anchored. Who knew where the pieces were? One wall was still standing, three walls were gone, and a toilet lay on its side. EcoQueen closed her eyes and willed all the damaged appliances scattered around to come toward her. Pieces too big for even two humans to lift together dragged along and over the piles toward her as if she was a powerful magnet. Her posture was confident and stable, a stance that grounded her firmly. It was a superhero stance, strong and solid.

EcoQueen drew metal pieces toward her. Damaged refrigerators, ovens, microwaves, sinks, and busted air conditioners spun and converged around her like a sports team getting in a huddle. Lola could see the small electrical bolts coming out of EcoQueen's fingertips.

Kora was manipulating an electrical storm generated from her own body, a superpower she had finally perfected after thousands of hours of training. In her grounded stance, like someone trying not to get pushed over, she directed her opened palms at the spent metal shards of wasted house parts and appliances to stir the useless appliances into a soup. With subtle push and pull motions, her goal was to repurpose the fragments of destruction made from the hurricane into something that would be useful.

Lola's eyes widened while watching EcoQueen, who looked the same age as she was, about the same height—just a few inches over five feet. Small but fierce. This young stranger was conjuring up the focus to melt metal with her hands. It did not seem real, though it happened right in front of her eyes, and she filed it away with the trauma of what she had just experienced. A foreign girl melting metal did not seem as weird as maybe it should have, so she just watched and observed, without judgment or even trying to fit it into reality. The stress of the hurricane had numbed her to surprises.

EcoQueen melted the materials before her into a solid plate of metal and laid it down to rest on top of the concrete foundation, the only thing that remained of that house. EcoQueen put her arms down to her sides, having just expended all the superpower she could muster for that moment. She walked around it and looked pleased. Lola was still confused.

"OK? What exactly did you just do and how is this going to help?" Lola asked, impressed but not as satisfied as EcoQueen herself seemed to be.

"This should get you the energy you need. It's one big solar panel. Just wait a bit, and the sun will shine on it and turn the sun's energy into the power you need for your phone, fridge, water . . . the essentials."

"What? You just fashioned a solar panel somehow?" Lola asked.

"Yes. These solar cells will convert the sun's energy into power you can use right now. Here, help me prop it up so it is facing south, where it can get the most sunlight in a day. Oh, here is the clincher, you need one of these." She molded something the size and shape of a large pizza box. "It's the inverter. It takes the direct current from the photovoltaic solar panels and converts it into alternating current. And voilà, you can then charge your devices from it! Go find all the car batteries you can, plug them in here, and then you have a place to store the energy so you can use it when the sun is not shining. Day or night, you'll have power you can use."

Lola pulled her dead phone out of her pocket. She had lost her shoe, but somehow she held on to her phone and its charger. It had gotten a little wet, so she wondered if it would charge back up. It felt like a potential lifeline in the palm of her hand. She thought about her grandparents and hoped and prayed the phone would charge up so she could possibly make contact with them—and her best friend, Jasmine—to see if they survived the storm. Lola bent over, plugged in her phone, and waited. Hoping, praying, it would come back to life . . .

Sure enough, the charging signal activated with that reassuring lightning bolt in the tiny battery icon. She praised the sun and EcoQueen, who got it set up, as her cell phone vibrated, dinged twice, and became animated like a long-lost friend. The short lines came streaming in:

"We are OK."

"Where are you?"

"Tía Estella and I are OK."

That was all she needed to read to feel connected to the most loved people in her world, knowing they were somewhere out there, alive, also dealing with the aftermath of the storm in other parts of the island. It was reassuring to know that her people were safe, and everyone on the island was in this together.

Río, at mission control, saw the opportunity with the connection and quickly pressed the buttons on his keyboard, continents away, to help EcoQueen slip back through the radio waves like a cell phone call jumping from towers, back to her home in California.

CHAPTER 17

FAMILY TROUBLES

CALIFORNIA

After coming back from the hurricane mission, Kora couldn't stop thinking about all the daughters, all the other children who lost a parent to climate change, like she had. She ruminated and related with the pain they would feel, the sadness, the loss they would hold with them their whole lives, as she would. That connection was uniting, but also depressing. Kora couldn't stomach the thought of more loved ones lost to more families due to global warming events. The destruction from Mother Nature, or more accurately from humanity, who had pushed Nature past the breaking point, was hard enough for Kora to cope with. Now she was living with the feeling that her profound loss was not unique, and that grief like hers was rippling through devastated, climate-affected communities all over the world.

The day after her mission to the Caribbean, Río came through on her dad's iPad, which was sitting in the orchard of Apple devices charging on the hotel mini kitchen counter. This time, he wasn't giving her an emergency briefing and zipping her out to another climate disaster; he showed up for a much-needed counseling session. He knew exactly what she was feeling. Sometimes he had the hypersensory ability to feel the emotions of people he was interacting with, even virtually. It wasn't only because Kora was his twin, but because he had the confusing ability to absorb others' emotions. In some situations, he was not able to distinguish which emotions were his and which belonged to someone else. He just felt it all. And this could turn into emotional overwhelm sometimes, freezing him with an abundance of love or anger, joy or fear. He knew well enough that Kora was feeling sad and getting lost in the grief for her mother. He tried to console her, but all the wrong words came out. "If you are angry, then do something about it."

Kora knew he was trying, but this did not make her feel any better.

Then he said, "Don't worry, you still have our mom!"

This confused her even more. Her biological mother was a stranger, and she still didn't even know if she could trust Río's backstory. It didn't make much sense, and he could have created those graphs about their DNA, but she was enjoying the teletransport missions and couldn't wait for the next one. She decided to see if he could give her a little more insight into her powers.

"So, Río. You seem to know a lot more about me and EcoQueen than I understand. From that expedition where you dumped me in the ocean, I know I can breathe underwater. Can I fly?"

"No, sorry, can't do that, but I can get you to places around the world as quickly as email travels," Río said.

"I wish I could talk to animals, understand what they were thinking back to me. Can I have that superpower?" She thought about how much it would have meant to be able to know what went on in Zuma's head. Her heart broke a little more, thinking about him.

"Hmm, I'm not sure about interspecies communication. You can fix things, melt things, repair things, break things—anything with electricity. I know you were trained on how to harness your electricity. We are asking that you use it full strength. In the right place and time, you can save millions of lives being threatened by climate change right now!"

"Can I disappear? Can I shrink? Can I read minds?" She fantasized as she started to envision herself as a real superhero like in the comic books.

"I don't think those abilities are among EcoQueen's attributes." Río didn't sound at all disappointed, just matter-of-fact.

"Well, where can I go next to do what I can with what I've got, Río?" Kora was beginning to feel empowered when she was EcoQueen.

When she was on a mission, she was able to take action toward combatting the climate change problem that killed her mom. She couldn't wait to figure out what the next climate change event was so that she could hopefully help fix it. In her mind, if she could prevent one child from losing their mom to global warming, like she did, she was making a significant impact on the world. So she wanted to go.

"There is a mission in Cape Town, South Africa. Due to severe drought, the city is almost out of water," Río offered.

"Could you tell me a little more background? We've talked about droughts in my environmental science class, but let's do a quick briefing. I want to start brainstorming before I hit the ground."

Río and Kora shared what they knew about the situation and about droughts in general. The government of Cape Town, South Africa, had named the much-anticipated fearful day "Day Zero," which was a moving target not as to *if*, but *when*, the city would run out of the water in their reservoirs—and thus running from any faucet. The government had called for drastic water conservation measures for all 4.6 million residents of Cape Town, which was a modern city with all the amenities of a civilized and developed metropolis . . . but was also just days away from a critical humanitarian crisis for every single resident living there. Water rationing did not exclude the babies, the farmers, the elderly, or the hospitalized from the reality of the city's water supply running dry. Cape Town was in its fourth year of unprecedented drought. Higher-than-average temperatures were becoming routine, and the normal dependable rains had not bathed Cape Town in drenching and refreshing downpours as they used to. The city's four main reservoirs, the population's primary water source, relied on rainfall, which had not been delivered from the heavens in over 365 consecutive days. No rain—no drinking water for anyone who resided in the municipality of Cape Town.

A year ago they had begun to truck in bottled water from afar, which was not sustainable. This was the first time in modern history that a major metropolitan area could feasibly run out of clean drinking water for its entire population. A crisis of epic proportions was predicted should the city fail to conserve the last drops of water available in their reserves. And each day they prayed for rain as the clay earth got drier and drier, parched and harder than rock, void of any moisture holding the soil together.

"Now that you have been briefed, are you ready to go, EcoQueen?"

"I was born ready, Río."

Río typed in the destination. "OK, coordinates are S 33°55'7.89" and E 18°25'23.88". All you have to do is place your fingers on Control, E, and Q. EcoQueen, you are good to go."

Kora placed her hands softly and nervously on the keys, and the mission began. She was sucked in through the LCD screen and transported to a place where climate catastrophe knocked at the door.

CHAPTER 18

DAY ZERO

CAPE TOWN, SOUTH AFRICA

EcoQueen fell out of an older-generation PC computer on the desk in a room that was sparsely furnished and hot. A window was open, with no screen, and the white curtain blew inward. The walls were painted white and cracked in places, the floor was concrete, and there was a single bed. She picked herself off the bedroom floor.

Even though she was a superhero now, she still had not perfected a smooth exit when she came flying through another computer screen somewhere foreign to her. But since this was only her third mission, she didn't waste any time feeling bad about it. She dusted herself off and got stable on her legs. She took the superhero stance with arms on hips and her chest puffed up. That helped her confidence.

EcoQueen glanced back at the monitor.

Río typed to her: "Water Crisis, Cape Town, Day Zero looms. The city will soon run out of water. You are on it."

Feeling a dip in her confidence, EcoQueen exhaled loudly.

"Seriously? What am I supposed to do about that? I can't invent water. I really don't think I can fix this one, Río." This was a different kind of emergency. There would be no quick fix. This was a long, drawn-out problem, and even though she and Río had talked through the situation, she worried that she couldn't help Cape Town. She hoped that inspiration would strike.

A woman in a different part of the house called out, "Nelson, it's your turn to take a bath!"

A boy's voice from down the hallway responded, "That's OK, Mom, I jumped in the ocean today. I rinsed off, I feel clean."

"OK, then call your brother. I don't think he's bathed in over a week now. He can use this morning's dishwater for his bath. I put it in the tub before I went to work."

EcoQueen peeked out into the rest of the house. Down the hallway, she caught a quick glimpse of a middle-aged woman putting down a bag of groceries and a few big water bottles while simultaneously kicking off her uncomfortable high heels from work, transitioning to mommying just like that.

Never did Nelson's mom, Amahle, think in her whole life growing up in Cape Town that she would be living like this, anxiously studying the containers of the finite amount of water that was available for her family. Their only water for the week sat on the breakfast room table in seven one-gallon plastic jugs. Scarcity had set in for real.

EcoQueen saw the boy, Nelson, who looked like he was in his early teens, getting a towel ready for his brother in the bathroom. He called out, "Tonio! Bath time!"

Tonio, who looked to be about five years old, marched from the kitchen toward the bathroom, where Nelson awaited. Tonio stepped out of his red soccer shorts and dirty tank top to let them drop lifeless in a pile next to the bathtub before he hustled into it. The bath seemed oversize compared to his small body. There was less than two inches of water sitting in the basin, which was clearly not enough to fully submerge any part of little Tonio's body. Actually, it wasn't even enough to cover the top of his foot. He sat in the puddle-size bathwater and scooped what he could into a plastic measuring cup to drip water over himself. Nelson handed him the towel, stiff from air-drying, and helped Tonio give himself a brisk rubdown before he changed into a fresh outfit.

As the boys exited the bathroom, EcoQueen took a quick evasive maneuver by dropping to the floor and rolling under Nelson's neatly made bed.

The older boy sat down in front of the monitor EcoQueen had entered through. Río had deleted traces of their communications, so

Nelson navigated to the City of Cape Town web page without any sus-
picions that a superhero was hiding in his room.

Nelson called out, "Mom, now they're saying that Day Zero will
begin within the week. The reservoir is at 25 percent capacity." He
whispered to himself, "Our city is out of water."

Nelson had become obsessed with his personal responsibility to
his family, his neighborhood, and his city in the collective effort to conserve water. He kept cranking on his neck to try to crack it, a nervous
habit he recently adopted because of the stress of the real possibility of
actually running out of water. He sucked down another soda, cautious
not to drink his allotted amount of drinking water. The responsibility
to try and save every drop of water available for his little brother and
mom weighed heavily on him. Water was the clear lifeblood to their
survival. He could not understand how any living thing could go on
living without water. The drought crisis brought a real doomsday kind
of feeling.

They used to be able to turn on the faucet for showering, for wash-
ing dishes, clothes, and cars—using what they needed and letting the
overflow vanish down the drain. Since warnings of Day Zero loomed,
Nelson would go with his mom every Tuesday after school to a place that
had recently required armed guards—a local natural spring trickling
out of a mountainside. It was a source where Amahle's grandparents
had gone for clean drinking water before the city got modern plumb-
ing. Nelson and his mom would fill up their ration of two one-gallon
jugs per family member. It was hard to carry, but once they got it home,
it was their lifeline. This was as much water as a toilet in the US used
each flush, but during Day Zero, this is how much Nelson's family had
to spread out for a week. The line at what was once a secret spring
was now usually at least a one-and-a-half-hour wait. And the tension
always felt like a fight over water was about to break out. They say the
next wars will be over water, not oil, and Nelson believed it.

Usually, wealthy people were the ones who were the worst at conserving. When Nelson was a little kid, he used to play in the sprinklers,
was taught to flush each time he went to the bathroom, and his mom
made him take a bath every single night before bed. She would say,
"Nelson, you must wash the day's dirt off you so you can start school
again fresh, clean, and ready to learn." Sometimes he thought this was

the biggest waste of time when he could have been outside playing soccer with his friends in his neighborhood instead of sitting still getting
clean in a bath when he was just going to get dirty all over again the
next day. Back then, it made no sense to him. He had worn a fresh uniform to school every day that was washed and ironed twice a week! He
got a packed lunch bag and surely never had to worry about his next
drink of water during those times. But now, in his short fourteen years
of life, everything had changed. He was seeing the difference of what it
was like to have something and have it slowly taken away.

Some of the customs he learned as a younger boy had to be
unlearned as the family adapted to the real water-shortage crisis that
had hit his hometown. Now, he was expected not to flush the toilet
until it had been used so many times the stink became almost unbearable. They didn't run water over their toothbrush to get it wet; instead,
they dunked it in a cup, then used that same water to rinse. No longer
was drinking only half the water in your glass allowed. Now every drop
was counted and considered the source of survival. Water was life, and
they were slowly dehydrating.

Nelson sat at his computer, fixated on Day Zero information, gazing into the words, images, and videos on his screen and hoping that it
would make him feel better, but really it made him more anxious.

He researched the symptoms of dehydration. He puckered his
mouth and licked his lips to try and get more saliva going. He thought
about it, and he hadn't peed since the morning. He tried to swallow,
and it felt like drinking sand. The last thing he had read was "How long
can a person stay alive without drinking water?" The search results
told him "three to four days." He suddenly felt the symptoms acutely.
He ran to the kitchen and slurped down probably more than his allotted share of drinking water for the day. He had been so careful to take
less than that for weeks, but he finally cracked. And then, of course,
the guilt crept in, as the gallon jug looked desperately lower and much
more empty than before, and he had to wait a full six more days before
it could be filled again.

Nelson walked back into his room and wiped his eyes, still feeling
disoriented and dazed from mild dehydration. Was he seeing things? A
five-foot-two brown-skinned teenage girl in a green and blue spandex
superhero suit with built-in leotard over tights plus cape, belt, boots,

long straight black hair down to her butt, and turquoise armbands was in his room? Surely he was hallucinating. He did go through a comic book superhero phase when he was younger. . . . This couldn't be real. He rubbed his eyes.

EcoQueen had popped out of her hiding spot to read some of the up-to-the-minute information from Nelson's computer aloud to Río. Río was so pleased that his self-taught coding skills plus the algorithm and the software he created were running smoothly that he got out of his beloved swivel desk chair to jump up three times beside it, pumping his fist. He was confident that together with EcoQueen on the scene, as well as local activists also hard at work, he could innovate the way out of this environmental crisis.

Now that she realized Nelson was back in the room, instead of trying to hide again, EcoQueen planted her feet on the floor and got into the stance she had learned about in karate and public speaking, the supergirl stance, with her hands on hips, confident—the cape flying behind her. She tried to feel it, but then the self-doubt kicked in. She mumbled back to Río through the microphone in her lowered hood, "I have electrical powers, Río, I can't invent water for these people. I wish I could!"

Río replied in writing on Nelson's monitor: "They are at the brink of an environmental crisis and you have the power to reverse it. You know you do! Get creative. Think."

EcoQueen felt like she should do the polite thing and introduce herself to the person whose room she'd annexed as her Cape Town HQ. "Hello, Nelson! I'm EcoQueen. How do you think I can help with the drought?"

"Hmm, can you make rain clouds?" Nelson suggested. If a superhero shows up in your bedroom, you might as well talk to her.

"I'm kind of new to this gig, but . . . no, I don't think so. If only we could drink salt water, there is that great big wet ocean right there." She knew from her love of geography that Cape Town was where two oceans blended (the Atlantic Ocean and the Indian Ocean). So much water right there, and nothing to drink!

Río had been listening in. He hadn't been able to make the speakers loud enough for Nelson and EcoQueen to both hear, and he knew how it could feel to be left out of a conversation, so he kept typing his communications. He figured that would keep everyone brainstorming in Cape Town in the loop.

"Hang on, I have an idea. EcoQueen, I am sending you somewhere else so you can solve this problem. Nelson, do not freak out." He cranked on the keyboard on his desk in a frenzy of opening and closing pages, knocking out code, checking in with the satellite images and other data input.

Letter by letter, words appeared on the screen that reflected off EcoQueen's green eyes, finally writing out, "Get ready, EcoQueen."

As quickly as EcoQueen had popped into Nelson's room in Cape Town, she was gone.

CHAPTER 19

PLASTIC SOUP

SOUTH ATLANTIC PLASTIC GYRE

EcoQueen came up for air and looked around to get her bearings. This was her least favorite part of teletransport travel. She had no idea exactly where she would end up, and it took a few minutes for her senses to catch up and catch on. Even though Río was coaching her through the speakers in her superhero suit, it was still disorienting at first, even for a superhero. She kept getting thrown into the middle of disasters. She still needed to use her brains, to figure out what to do. Superpowers without logic and reason have no power at all. Knowledge and power needed to be combined, and it took EcoQueen what felt like a few minutes to gather her thoughts and senses once she let go of the fiber-optic line where it crisscrossed the bottom of the ocean floor.

Free of the line, she slowly rose toward the surface. Salt water splashed into her nose and eyes and mouth, and it stung her eyeballs. There was also a short delay to allow for her superhero suit to adapt to the new environment. She was so thirsty, but all the water around her could not quench her thirst.

"Ocean water covers 80 percent of the earth, but you can't drink it to survive," Río chimed in, knowing that she was thirsty. A strange combination to be wet and surrounded by water but not able to hydrate.

The ocean she bobbed in had a warm, pleasant, tropical feeling. She heard birds overhead barking at each other in a frenzy, dive-bombing from above to scoop up and eat whatever was floating around her. The sun was intense, and there were no people or buildings visible, just a flat horizon line where water met the sky. After a few minutes of floating there, treading water, she spun around in a complete circle but saw nothing but rolling blue-green ocean water. It registered that she was somewhere in an ocean, in a subtle current that was winding up on itself.

"OK, Río. So now I'm in a warm ocean floating with a bunch of plastic." Pieces of plastic, big and small, were bobbing with her in all directions and floated below her. It went on for miles, actually—a plastic soup in the middle of the ocean.

Río helped orient her, answering her unspoken question: *Where am I?* "You are in the Great South Atlantic Plastic Gyre."

When Kora studied the colorful bits on the top layer, she could see what their temporary once- or twice-use purpose had been: a toothbrush, a ziplock bag, a flip-flop, a hair clip, a Q-tip, a tooth flosser, a plastic water bottle, various caps to countless other plastic bottles, a straw, remnants of some Lego, a lighter. She was adrift among plastic trash that had all found its way to that spot, traveling on a current. You name it—if it was plastic, it was there in a colorful speckled plastic soup stewing in the sun, congregating in a mass the size of Texas. There were also bits that no longer resembled their single-use virgin form but had broken down enough to be the size of the colorfully painted pebbles you find in a fish tank. She'd read about these, that there was actually a term for them: nurdles—new vocabulary invented to describe tiny bits of lentil-size plastics in the ocean.

Pieces brushed against her legs and got in her hair. There were some big chunks printed with letters in different scripts and languages, which had clearly drifted from faraway lands to this unnatural convergence of all things plastic. EcoQueen grabbed a big hunk of something floating by. It was sturdy and thick; she figured it must have been part of a car or boat before it spent the rest of its life bobbing there. She pulled her body up and used it as a raft to assess the scene, getting a view a bit above the surface of the sea for more perspective.

She had never seen so much plastic in one place at one time, and she had been to a landfill before. She wondered how and why it had all ended up here, in the ocean floating like a contaminated cesspool, and why nobody was doing anything about it. But perhaps she could. Maybe that was why Río sent her there, delving into one environmental disaster in order to solve another one in Cape Town.

EcoQueen thought about Nelson taking a big drink of water.

The seabirds overhead were in a frenzy. They sounded like a conference of grumpy married couples barking at each other in disagreeable arguments. But then, one at a time, each seabird would plunge from above and scoop up a beak full of whatever was floating around EcoQueen. The birds were going for these fun-looking bite-size pieces thinking they were food. They looked just like fish eggs, but were actually petrochemical pellets. "I don't think you should be eating this stuff, birds," EcoQueen yelled up. "This is not food for you! It's plastic. Not edible! Not good. You can't digest it!" But then she remembered she didn't have that animal communication superpower she ordered up. Alas, she could not get them to stop ingesting dangerous plastic. She only had electrical powers. So how was she going to use that in the midst of all this plastic?

Río filled her in with the kind of facts he loved pulling up. In his almost-robotic, flat reading voice, he quickly got her up to speed with some research. She listened through her hood. He recited, "Since humans started their love affair with plastic around the 1960s, the stream of plastic into the environment has been steady. Plastics became so cheap to produce and so versatile, almost our entire existence became centered around plastics, and humans have produced more than they can handle."

He got a hint of satisfaction that he could come up with facts about any kind of science and history, right there at his fingertips. His search engine was a tool, he knew, if he held it right.

EcoQueen's mind wandered to the origin story of this plastic that came to rest here in the sea. What was most identifiable were the plastic water bottles, everywhere. Then her eyes scanned to a yellow laundry detergent container, a somewhat deteriorated Barbie doll, and a piece to a broken plastic beach chair that floated nearby. A wet grocery plastic bag wrapped around EcoQueen's leg. She flinched; the feeling was worse than a real jellyfish on her body. Diapers were ballooned, heavy and saturated, alongside to-go cups, toys. Her heart broke seeing the scope and breadth of the pollution.

What was she going to do with all this? She thought about Bodi, the first time she met him on the beach, picking up trash and recycling, his Sunday morning church alternative.

EcoQueen yelled out to Río, the only person who had any idea where she was, alone in the middle of the Atlantic Ocean. "What happened to recycling? Why is all of this here in the first place? Where did it all come from, and how did it get so bad?"

Again, Río quickly spouted info, maybe too much for the moment, but EcoQueen got a quick lesson on her questions.

Río said, "Leo Hendrik Baekeland is not a household name, but it should be. He was a Belgian chemist who made the laboratory breakthrough in 1907 that would change the stuff our world is made of. He was heating up some chemicals and accidentally plastic was born—an element of a thousand uses."

Río continued, "In 2018, nearly 359 million metric tons of plastic were produced. So much that we don't know what to do with all the single-use excess waste at this point. Over 1.15 million tons of plastic are entering the ocean each year from rivers, and there are now five gyres in the different parts of the oceans, each swirling as its own body of plastic mass. And you are in one of them."

"How in the world is anyone going to be able to clean all of this up, Río? Am I supposed to figure out a way to suck all this plastic out of the ocean? It is everywhere! Impossible, sorry!"

But then EcoQueen considered her options.

I guess I could MELT it, and repurpose all the plastic into something helpful instead of harmful? she thought to herself. *It will never biodegrade, so it will last forever. I could recycle it into something useful.* It was as if she had an endless supply of material—an artist's unlimited palette floated around her to make something new.

Her original mission in Cape Town came back into her mind. Those people in Cape Town needed drinking water more than anything else in the world right now. *Water, water everywhere but not a drop to drink,* she thought again, starting to feel a salty sunburn just under her eyes. Her thirst built, causing an ache in her salivary glands, and she wished for just a sip of clean, potable water.

Everything lined up like the pots of gold on a slot machine, and the answer came in loud and clear. She hesitated no more.

"I've got it! I see how this is all connecting now!" The wheels in her mind and powers were rolling now.

She started the chi gung concentration of her breath, and it focused her energy through her fingertips. When she got into this state, every other distraction fell off the planet. She had gotten so good at dropping into her superpower space, it no longer felt like work or practice. The skill had become automated. Making a practice a habit allowed her brain to do things without even thinking about it. She had come a long way since her practices on the beach with Ms. Piper.

As the electricity started radiating from her and out of her finger-tips, the plastic gyre started spiraling and merging in closer to her like a crowd at a concert when the band starts playing. Her arms were in the air overhead, looking like she was about to conduct a symphony of plastic bits that converged in front of her. She made the plastic gyre spin faster and faster until it began to lift off the surface of the water like a vinyl record on a turntable. Then she started to heat it up. She had to get the electricity from her hands up to 491 degrees Fahrenheit in order to melt the plastic into another form. The individual pieces started to blend into each other, swirling into a rainbow river of melted plastic. Plastic attracted more plastic, adding to the surface area of this liquid plastic plate.

Spinning and tossing the plastic molten lava mass like pizza dough, she kept adding to it, expanding it, transforming it, creating it into a plastic island. Once she released it, it sat atop the ocean surface like a landing strip. The mass was the size of Bishop Rock, the smallest island in the world, at eight thousand square feet. This new island made of plastic was fortified, strong, and sturdy. In making it, EcoQueen had bonded together every little nurdle with the big chunks of plastic, too. The island cooled, becoming stable and solid.

EcoQueen hoisted herself up on the new island, which looked like a floating plastic dock, and stood on it. She walked to the edges, and was pleased with the foundation she created. It was the size of twenty city blocks and untippable, solid as plastic could be, twenty feet thick in places. Usually, only volcanoes created new islands these days. Yet, this mound of plastic was big and sturdy. She could barely feel the motion of the ocean beneath it. A new artificial landmass had been formed, and the cleanup was considerable. As she gazed out onto the surface of the gyre, she seemed to have made a dent in the floating mess.

EcoQueen readied for the next phase—to make more water drinkable. It would take a bit of engineering! Río liked what she was thinking and found a 3D blueprint online. He sent the computerized architectural design plan over to the processors in her suit to read. Repurposing the plastic to use in the spools of material needed to make a new object was brilliant in this situation. She could use her heat and her fingertips as the printer to melt and deposit the perfect design.

"Time to transform a problem into a solution!" she said aloud. From the image in her head, she used her hands and the melting electric powers to configure a whole machine . . . a water desalination plant that would sit atop the floating island and could make salt water drinkable, using heat to evaporate water and then recapturing the fresh water for people to drink and use. All she needed to make now were some holding tanks.

She began to mold pipes that looped back on themselves like a trumpet. She formed pressure gauges, basins, and storage tanks, more tubes, a membrane, a filter—without thinking, she followed the uploaded design. It was fun, like she was spraying silly string as she layered the plastic material to erect an entire desalination plant atop the plastic island. Eight million tons of plastics are leaked into the ocean every year, about a garbage truck a minute, but she figured she had cleaned up at least a year's worth of plastic for this project. She had heard the prediction that in twenty years there will be more pieces of plastic in the sea than fish, so she felt proud helping to remove it. But she couldn't forget Cape Town. *Focus on the water . . .*

Río entered the coordinates for the offshore location where the new aircraft carrier–size water desalination plant would go, and through drone navigation, off it went. To stave off Day Zero. A gift from the sea and EcoQueen. Río notified the coast guard of the invention, so they were expecting it. People from Cape Town went out to greet the potable-water-making island and shepherd the life-saving machine near shore. They just had to plug it into the city's power grid, and clean water would be ready at the making. Ta-da! Water for all.

That took care of most of the visible plastic floating around in that part of the ocean, even though it wasn't fully cleaned. *What else could I recycle all the smaller bits of plastic into that would serve a greater purpose?* EcoQueen thought to herself from the remainder of the Great South Atlantic Gyre.

EcoQueen knew there had been an unprecedented surge in the number of displaced people, which had reached about 70.8 million worldwide in 2018. Hurricanes like Katrina in New Orleans could displace more than a million people with one storm, and then there were all those evacuated from wildfires, tsunamis, war, drought, and rising sea levels. Climate refugees were a real thing, and there were people running from disasters with nowhere to go and certainly no house to live in if it had been destroyed by a natural event.

As she pondered, EcoQueen corralled more and more of the plastic. She used her energy flow to turn it and churn it.

I could make emergency shelters out of the melted plastic. It would just take a few walls and a roof. The plastic could be made into a building material to create homes for all the climate refugees in the world who had to flee their homes because of devastation and destruction. These shelters could keep the elements out and be used as temporary houses for the millions of people around the globe who were homeless, many from the devastating effects of rising seawaters. *Heck, my dad and I could use one, we're still living in a hotel! I'll make some rectangular houses out of this plastic—walls, floor, roof, and places for windows.*

She zapped a few together and loaded a tanker with shelter for at least five hundred families. That was not enough, but it was something.

"I'm out. That was plenty for one day of work. Río, take me back, please!" she yelled into the air.

"Dive down. You have to grab onto the fiber-optic line. Extraction sequence is ready when you are," he responded.

She moved like a dolphin and splashed her feet above her in order to get down deep. EcoQueen grabbed the line that crisscrossed the ocean's flow for connectivity between continents, and took the ride back home.

CHAPTER 20

ROOTS

CALIFORNIA

Although Kora was fully committed to her work as EcoQueen, she was still very curious about Río's claim to be her long-lost twin. On the weekend, after she and Bodi had done their homework and took a bike ride, she decided to do a little investigating into her own past. She asked her father if she could get access to their storage unit, to dig through all the things salvaged from their home. Kora hoped that something from her mother's paperwork might lead her to information that could confirm she might have another family in Australia.

Kora's dad had given her keys to the storage unit without hesitation. She thought maybe Duncan had been glad to know that she'd be out of the house for the morning, so he could work uninterrupted on the weekend and without any dad guilt.

As she poked around in the moving boxes the cleanup crews had put the remnants of her family's life in after the smoke and sprinkler damage from the fire, Kora felt the loss deep in her gut. There were her mother's favorite twenty-year-old, broken-in Frye cowboy boots that she would wear when feeling "back to earthy." Kora picked up the small flowerpots she had painted for her mom's kitchen windowsill herb garden for Mother's Day in middle school. She stumbled across Zuma's second-favorite squeaky hedgehog toy. All these memories had been reduced to smoke-tarnished, water-stained rubbish that she and her dad hadn't been able to face since the fire.

Kora rummaged through a box mostly filled with kitchen implements, but some of her mom's jewelry and belts, too. None of this seemed helpful in Kora's quest for her origins. She lifted out a squashed shoebox to see what it might hold.

Inside were a few manila envelopes. They were folded in half to fit, but when Kora saw "Agencia de Adopción Los Árboles" written in her mom's confident handwriting, she stopped in her tracks. Something resonated in her, and she knew that she needed to spend more time going through these, but not there, not in the dank storage locker. She slipped the contents of the shoebox into her backpack.

She raced over to Bodi's on her bike. As she and Bodi sat in his living room, Kora slid the envelopes out of her backpack.

"Bodi, want to do some investigating with me?"

He smiled his ever-ready grin. "Of course! What is this?"

"I think it's all the paperwork from the adoption agency in Ecuador." She started unfolding the envelopes. Each had her mom's handwriting and the adoption agency name, and some had dates from the months leading up to the trip that brought Kora home to California with them.

The friends each started opening envelopes and scanning through the papers inside. It felt like unwrapping countless little gifts. Mostly it was copies of paperwork Blythe had submitted. She was always so proud of her ability to be a boss at bureaucratic paper shuffling, a skill she learned at her corporate job that translated nicely into the adoption process. Kora loved seeing her mom's handwriting again and again, proof of how much work Blythe had been willing to do to make Kora her own. One paper had some notes in Spanish about weight, length, vaccinations—doctor's notes from when Kora was a baby in the orphanage.

At the bottom of an envelope that contained Blythe's and Duncan's passports and printouts of plane tickets and hotel confirmations, Kora felt an unusual weight. When she upended the envelope and tapped the bottom, out slid what looked like a handmade bracelet covered in small, round beads—a perfect match to the bracelet she'd seen on Río's wrist on their video calls before every mission they'd done together.

Bodi could tell this artifact from Kora's childhood held a special resonance for his best friend. This was the only thing she'd ever
touched that came from her life before Blythe and Duncan welcomed
her into their family. Bodi said quietly, "I'll go make us some smoothies, OK?" to excuse himself and give Kora some time to process what
these discoveries meant.

She tied the woven fiber around her left wrist, the same wrist Río
wore his bracelet on. As soon as she tightened the knot, she felt a diz-
zying disorientation, and the scratchy rug below her seemed to melt
away, replaced by warm, loamy ground.

**

When Avalon finally got to the rainforest, after days of travel, she said
to her local research contact, Joaquin, "I am looking to replicate this
jungle in a controlled environment. Do you know which species here
are the most productive in removing carbon from the atmosphere?"
Pollution was not cleaning itself up on its own out there in the world,
especially in China, where her project was based. "I am growing a
hydroponic rainforest indoors, in a controlled environment, with no
soil. It cleans the air, like yours does here, but in the city. Can you point
out plants that you think would be resilient enough for transport?"

Joaquin was intrigued. He could sense Avalon was motivated.
Ecotourists came and went, but he was fascinated by Avalon: a twenty-
five-year-old powerhouse—motivated, intelligent—with a PhD, a cute
Australian accent, and a determined manner. She wore a well-worked
Australian wide-brimmed Akubra hat, and her untamed sandy-blond
curls unfurled from beneath it, going every which way. A natural turquoise stone dangled from a leather string around her neck, and a silver cuff curved around her wrist. She was sweating profusely in the
humid jungle, but not embarrassed in the least bit by the moisture
rings in her armpits.

"I will show you whatever you need to know," Joaquin told her.
They started walking away from the research center. In fewer than one
hundred paces they were already exploring deep in the jungle.

Joaquin put on his guide voice and said what he told all the scientists that came to his forest: "For years experts have known that

the Amazonian rainforest functions like the lungs of Mother Earth, cleansing the carbon dioxide from the atmosphere and generating more than 20 percent of the oxygen we breathe. At one time rainforests covered 14 percent of the earth, but thanks in large part to human activity, they now cover less than half of that area—6 percent. If we continue at this rate, all rainforests could be destroyed in less than forty years, obliterating a whole ecosystem."

Avalon asked in her inquisitive singsong Australian accent, "Do you have a tree here similar to the Spekboom tree, from the Eastern Cape of Africa? The Spekboom can store solar energy to perform photosynthesis at night, and I am looking for another tree with similar enormous carbon-storing capabilities."

"Ah, good question, let's go meet the trees. Here, our biggest carbon sink is the Brazil nut tree." Scientists came all the time to his science center, but Joaquin could tell this scientist was special, different—intriguing.

The love for the rainforest and the fascination for the interconnectedness of it all seemed to sew their passions together. Joaquin's hands-on understanding and Avalon's deep technical command of all things earth science connected them in an authentic way, where they felt like they understood each other in a way that they had never experienced before.

Avalon's first love would always be with the world of scientific research. Studying science filled her up, excited her, and pulled her in, which made her feel purposeful and gave her pleasure. She had devoted her life to it. Yet, everything about Joaquin soon was on the forefront of her mind; she couldn't believe that such a crush actually developed between them, and she let it.

There was something magnetic about Joaquin. Yes, the green eyes, his biceps, his braids, and his smooth skin, the color of healthy, life-giving soil, were attractive, but she was also falling in love with his knowledge of the natural world around them. She loved how he observed, listened, and studied what was before him. He knew volumes. She wanted to be able to think like he did and feel that visceral connection to the rainforest in the way only someone born into it could.

The physical attraction came out of nowhere. Avalon was more bookish than seductive, but this man flipped a switch in her, and all she could think about was him. She studied how he moved and intentionally tried to get her body closer to his, wishing he would brush up against her each time he passed. They seemed to have a natural awareness around each other, like an effortless dance. She noticed that he faced her directly when he talked to her and looked thoroughly at her when he was listening. The eye contact was validating, and the slightly longer-than-usual glances were comfortable. The chemistry was real. Accented English, Spanish phrases, and Latin scientific names delivered out of his plump and wide smiling lips made her want to lean in more.

He would say, "Come, I'll show you!" and guide her hand as they walked deeper together into the dense rainforest confidently, although she had lost her bearings already.

He caught a baby bird, a must-see multicolored crimson and topaz, to show her and melt her heart even more. "Look, Avalon," he said, holding it in the palm of his hand.

"What kind is it?" Her scientific, classifying mind defaulted to the practical question.

"This is a baby hyacinth macaw, getting rare because people hunt them for the pet trade. It will grow up to be one of the larger birds of the rainforest."

Avalon smiled and ran one finger down its soft wing.

Joaquin looked up, meeting her eyes.

***

"Kora? Kora? Are you OK?!"

Kora snapped back into the reality of Bodi's living room. Two homemade smoothies were perched precariously on the coffee table's edge, where Bodi had hurriedly put them down as soon as he saw Kora sprawled on the floor next to their piles of papers.

"I'm fine. But feeling a little light-headed . . ." Kora sat up and leaned against the sofa.

"Drink this." Bodi pushed one of the smoothies into her hand and rubbed her back. "Just a sec." He stepped away for a minute, then sat down next to her on the rug and put a metal straw in the drink for her.

She drank tentatively at first, then with relish. "Mmm! Lots of blackberries in this!" The color came back to her cheeks. Then she remembered that Bodi had taken her out to forage the berries a few weeks after her mom's death to help her get away from Duncan's negativity, and a lump of grief and gratitude formed in her throat. They'd washed and frozen them together. Bodi knew how much she loved blackberries in her smoothies.

"Do you want to talk about it?" Bodi asked.

"I'm so worn out from school, and my trip to Cape Town, and now this. I think maybe I'm just overwhelmed. I think I'll head home and take a nap. Could we touch base tomorrow?"

"Sure! I'll swing by around nine. Maybe we can go grab a vegan breakfast taco at the food truck? How about I bike home with you?"

"Thanks, Bodi. That sounds perfect."

CHAPTER 21

CHILL OUT

THE ARCTIC

It was October, but in the Arctic, the temperature hit ninety, breaking records from as long as there had been recorded weather history. The area where the Greenland ice shelf had been frozen in place for more than a million years was melting into the sea. Where a down jacket and gloves were the normal gear, surf shorts and flip-flops could be donned on that abnormally balmy day. It continued to swelter in an unprecedented heat wave. With winter just around the corner, temperatures would usually be plunging, but this year they were not, and the ice sheets in the Arctic that usually headed into their deep freeze were not even getting close. The Arctic Ocean had not refrozen at all, setting a new record for the latest delay in ice formation the sea had ever experienced.

Río knew something needed to be done in this area of the world. Yet another climate disaster, so no break for EcoQueen. He would have to reach out to Kora. She must have been feeling like a doctor on call in the intensive care unit as new patients kept being wheeled in. This was not right, not normal, and not good for the earth or the Arctic. Río had been studying the climate emergency from headquarters: up all night, synthesizing data like he did, gazing into the blue light of his computer screens without registering life outside of his information world. His green eyes dived deeper into the pages open on the screen. He was submerged mentally and emotionally into the information he was taking in. Sometimes he wished he could unplug, but he had never practiced that skill, so it was nearly impossible to step away. He bounced his right knee, unaware, as if the motion was recharging his motor. It was as if it wasn't food or sunlight that energized him, it was data and problem-solving.

If the Arctic ice melted completely, it would have a ripple effect on the planet, causing the sea level to rise anywhere in the world where there was a coastline. Such a rate of rise would put four hundred million people around the world at risk of flooding every year. The water's edge would kiss the shores three to six feet higher than where it came now. Río's computer simulation showed which cities would be gulped up by the ocean. Neighbors miles away from the coast would be the newest owners of beachfront property, as all the others who had houses there would be forced to relocate because their land would be submerged.

Río contacted Kora in the kitchen, through one of her dad's tablets on the counter behind her as she worked with pen and paper at the dinner table/desk. "EcoQueen, can you hear me? You have to go to the Arctic, right now."

Kora put down her pen and sighed. She walked closer to the tablet so she could see Río. "Right this minute? I'm in the middle of an essay."

"Yes, EcoQueen . . . This time, I'm going to send an interface that will be safe for you to touch. When you see the EcoQueen button appear on this touch screen, use your left index finger."

Kora touched the EcoQueen logo that appeared on her dad's tablet.

EcoQueen entered the Arctic research center through a computer in one of the few buildings in the area. The scientists were out, observing something that they had never seen before: autumnal waterfalls and rivers that had developed overnight from the ice melting during this record-breaking season. They watched ancient ice melt to water and mix with the sea. The ten scientists who lived and studied there all felt an anxious and fearful pit in their stomachs as they observed what they were studying vanish before them, and individually they knew what this would mean for the planet. EcoQueen swiftly exited the Arctic research lab where she arrived on the scene and stepped outside into the tundra. The sun was so bright reflecting off the white snow and ice that she pushed a button on her suit to insert protective contact lenses for the expedition.

A lone skinny polar bear walked by, looking weak and confused. His environment was changing so dramatically. He lumbered in the uncharacteristic heat.

EcoQueen's suit cooled her off in air-conditioning mode rather than having to keep her warm as would have been expected in the Arctic. Everything was backward and upside down. The sensors Río designed for the suit reacted to what was real, and the reality was that it was uncomfortably hot in the Arctic, even for mammals without a polar bear's thick pelt.

The ice from the Greenland ice shelf had been melting at a rate seven times faster than it was twenty years ago and was being lost much quicker than climate scientists had predicted. The fact that it wasn't reforming as usual with the turn of the seasons was disastrous.

EcoQueen walked to the shelf and saw waterfalls. Glaciers that had been frozen in place for millennia broke off, releasing to splash into the ocean below, unattached from the bond of ice molecules through which they had clung in place for thousands of years. It was a beautiful sight, the ice-blue glacial waters free-falling, a mix of gravity and virgin pure water molecules rushing into ocean waters. But it was something ecotourists would venture out to witness in Bali or Costa Rica, somewhere tropical where waterfalls should happen, not the Arctic, where things are meant to be frozen in place. Ice should not be melting off at 324 billion tons per year.

At the end of the shelf, EcoQueen was careful not to stand too close, as huge pieces of ice were calving off in boulder-size chunks. They looked like ice cubes in a glass of soda sitting under the sun on a summer day, mixing with the ocean, soon to become one.

She spoke to Río. "I can't believe what I'm seeing. This is a major problem! What am I supposed to do here?" She scanned her brain, trying to come up with anything. It felt beyond her abilities to help. "They don't need any more heat here, that is for sure!"

What she recognized as twin synchronicity happened: the moment she had the inspiration for the solution, Río spoke to her from mission control. "The sun is beating down so warm on the ice, you have to block the sun for now," he said. "A day's reprieve can make a difference."

"I was thinking the same thing! I wish I could move mountains to shade the ice."

"How about creating shade?"

"How? Is there more plastic nearby that I could form into some sort of giant umbrella? I worry that melting that much plastic would take too much heat. It's so hot here already. . . ." Kora brainstormed out loud. She knew she needed to block the sun, but what could be fast and effective?

"With a cloud," Río said.

"I can do that? That could have been handy in South Africa."

"I don't think you can guarantee precipitation, but you could seed some clouds. You can use your powers to encourage them to plump up and at least be a barrier between the strong sun and the ice, for now! You just need to get the Arctic cool enough that the ice can refreeze when tomorrow's cold front moves in." The pace of Río's speech sped up. Excitedly, he pushed his fingers through his unbrushed black hair that fell over his face.

As she was waiting for some more data and thinking through her cloud-seeding plan, a strange monstrous sound screamed out of the ice, and then EcoQueen saw the crack. The spot she was standing on was cracking ten feet from the edge, where the Arctic Ocean splashed up against it. Stirring her hand over the churning sea, EcoQueen drew up the frigid Arctic waters to her palms, only to administer heat to essentially boil and evaporate the liquid away. What was left of the salt water when the water turned to vapor?

As EcoQueen turned her electrical energy up to the next level, the liquid evaporated away, and the salt clung to her hands. It looked like shaved-ice balls started to grow from the bottom of her palms. The salt crystals bonded in a crystalline structure of molecules of sodium and chloride ions. After she pulled the necessary mineral from the sea, she turned her hands from the position of gathering to offering.

It was exactly what EcoQueen needed for her next move. The salt mounds had grown to the size of snowman spheres. She launched them from her palms toward the heavens, aiming at the one minuscule wispy cloud in the upper atmosphere that was probably looking down at the ice shelf in despair. Instantaneously, the seeded cloud began to change. It split, grew, and plumped until the sky started to fill with what looked like puffy white cartoon clouds. They were soon joined by even more clouds drawing closer.

"Is it OK to mess with nature this way?" EcoQueen asked Río while she impregnated another cloud with salt, something natural but definitely added.

"Something needs to be done! The glaciers are melting. It is ninety degrees on the eightieth longitude in the Arctic today, and there is barely any more sea ice. You decide." Río, not so comfortable with philosophical conversation, always defaulted to data and research. He was able to communicate better in facts and could rapidly filter through research to form his response to any questions. "As the clouds suck up the salt crystals, they attract tiny particles of water, which collide and become heavier. Eventually the water might fall as rain, but today we don't want it to get to that point, we just want to help create more clouds. At times, silver iodide or dry ice have been used, which can help to increase the amount of heat radiated back into space and help cool a warming world. But from the ambient temperature gauges in your suit, I can tell that the sea salt you've used is doing a good job with clouds that are rapidly reducing the sun's melting effects."

"OK, I guess I am helping. The clouds are at least acting as a bit of a parasol to block out the beating sun, for now, for a little bit," EcoQueen said.

"I don't know how long the particles will stay in the air, but you've made a good quick fix. The weather station readouts indicate a cold front should move in tonight, so Arctic-appropriate weather should take over soon. Chances look good. This should hold things stable until the weather can get more ice back to frozen. Thank you, EcoQueen."

EcoQueen ran back to the research station and jumped back through the computer to California, which was still having its own climate problems. A rare thunder and lightning storm boomed, and large hail smacked down, adding little divots to her dad's unprotected BMW, parked in the hotel parking lot instead of his custom-designed garage at the Cliff House. In the most logical part of herself, Kora knew Duncan wouldn't appreciate her making connections between his work with power plants and this messed-up paint job. If losing his wife wasn't enough to help him change his life course, a few dents on his roof and hood wouldn't do the trick. But Kora couldn't help but hope that maybe he'd come around someday and appreciate her way of treading lightly on the earth—and EcoQueen's way of jumping in to save it.

CHAPTER 22

ACQUA ALTA

VENICE, ITALY

Kora was grateful to have a roof over her head, somewhere to call home, but she struggled to feel at home in the hotel. She realized that she was planning most of her hours trying to be away from "home"—at the beach, at Bodi's, or training with Ms. Piper. She tried to come back to the place she and her father were staying only to sleep.

Her dad never noticed what time she came home; he was usually there starting at seven, watching the news, and sipping on an adult beverage to unwind from the day. Sometimes when she key carded in the heavy hotel door, he didn't even seem to hear her come in. She understood that it was best to somehow get dinner for herself out, as he usually had a liquid dinner or ordered a pizza to the room. Sometimes she would say hi to him, and other times she would slip in, while his back was to the door, to change her clothes and slip out again. When her birthday came and went without even a word from her dad, she knew they were living in separate worlds.

What recharged Kora was nighttime rides on her bike, seeing only as far in front of her as her bike light would shine, pedaling faster and faster, so her heart was pumping, as she sang a song out loud that nobody could hear because she was whipping by so quickly. She was not self-conscious of someone hearing her. She knew the steepest hill in her neighborhood and, up in her seat, would hammer down on the pedals to get to the top of it, up to the view of the ocean. Watching the sunset there was what cleared her head.

Kora had started wearing the beaded bracelet she found among her adoption papers. She hadn't had any more out-of-body experiences from touching it, but she told Río about it and showed it to him on their debrief call after the Arctic ice mission. She asked Río how their parents met, and he confirmed what she had seen in her vision: that their mother, Avalon, and their dad, Joaquin, met on their mom's research trip to the Amazon.

Kora, Río, and Bodi were all excited that Kora had connected with her biological family.

When Río told Kora that EcoQueen was needed in Venice, Italy, she thought, *Perchè no?* Río could get EcoQueen anywhere with a few clicks—in time to offer some relief. Kora was intrigued by Venice, and had always dreamed of visiting the picturesque city, but not like this— during an emergency with evacuation orders in place.

EcoQueen waded through the plaza in the most significant sea level rise that the ancient city of Venice, Italy, had ever seen in its history. Venice had experienced *acqua alta* every year since the city was built in 400 CE, but this one was historically unprecedented and devastating, as the water rose in a way nobody was prepared for. It left plazas, lobbies, streets, and cafés swimmable, as the salty waters of the canals rose so high that walking was no longer possible, not even on the raised temporary boardwalks the city was used to setting up during the season of the highest tides. EcoQueen, once again, was delivered into a climate catastrophe because it was urgent and wildly destructive.

Río had been watching the satellite weather and had hacked into highly secure communications among members of the Italian Parliament to discover how big Venice's natural disaster was. Río was in the know regarding the moment-by-moment situation there, even though he was orchestrating the mission from his tidy, tech-filled bedroom in Australia. He rubbed his palms together in front of his face, like he always did when he was deep thinking and a million thoughts were going through his head at once. It was one of his processing habits, making heat in his hands, in order to try and sort his thoughts enough to do something with them.

The water reached EcoQueen's chest. Granted, she was petite, but the high waters were at historic levels. Luckily, she was a strong swimmer; if her feet could not touch the cobblestone street below the water, she could calmly switch to the breaststroke to continue to scout the scene. The perfect storm of high tide with uncharacteristic heavy rains and high winds flooded most of the city of canals under six feet of salt water.

EcoQueen remembered seeing a sign hoisted over the head of a girl her age at one of the various climate marches that had been going on around the world to try to raise climate change awareness. The poster, written in colored markers, read, "The Oceans Are Rising, and So Are We!"

Here it was, happening. There is nothing you can do to hold back the ocean. Humanity has tried, but the water always wins. Engineers had been working on flood barriers to protect the city, but this year they had been overrun. No matter what your superpower or higher power is, putting out your arms to block the flow of tidal waves will never work. Water does its own thing, and the people and the city had to retreat to higher ground while the ocean took over their streets. They had been warned. They all had been warned that if the climate kept warming, the sea levels would rise. The city was yet another victim of rising waters.

Another point for global warming, zero points for the people trying to stop this mess from happening! EcoQueen wondered how effective she could actually be with electrical powers to mitigate flooding. She stalled on her next move.

Water is essential to life and survival, yet water where you don't want it is utterly destructive. The salt water was seeping into the foundations of the city, corroding the columns that held it up for centuries, eating away at the mosaics that decorated it, the sculptures that told its stories in history.

EcoQueen's suit had been programmed this time for high performance in cool floodwaters. The material was set to the synthetic dolphin skin biomimicry texture function to give her insulation like that animal naturally had. Río was quite pleased with the functionality and how he could tweak its programming from mission control. Through the microphone and sensors in the hood of the suit, EcoQueen called out to Río for some more direction.

"Río, what am I supposed to do here? I have electrical superpowers, and electricity and water don't mix."

EcoQueen needed her bearings and some intel. Luckily, Río was prepared.

"Eighty-five percent of the city is underwater at the moment, and you may be helpful with drying it out. Think of a big hair dryer. Saint Mark's Basilica was hit super hard. You can go over there and try to help divert the water." Río was good at the play-by-play and logistics, as long as he had data to back him up. That was how his mind worked; his learning, thinking, and problem-solving abilities as a person on the autism spectrum translated into him being extremely gifted.

An empty gondola drifted by EcoQueen. Where just yesterday dogs were walking and street performers were filling the air with music, what had been sidewalk was now more canal, with five feet of ocean water moving with a powerful current. Land had turned to lagoon. But now was not the time for sightseeing. There was work to do, and EcoQueen finally understood why she was there. She waded in the dragging, delayed walk that happens when your legs are surrounded by water.

When she reached the front door of the basilica church, she was moved by the holiness of the place. She felt unexpectedly spiritual in the light shining through the stained glass, surrounded by each carefully placed mosaic tile hanging on the walls—barely hanging on, like everything else. The severity of the situation hit her. This beloved building, which had been a gathering place for centuries, could easily be destroyed beyond repair in the next twenty-four hours as a result of the damaging water that had poured in. Not just this one, but half of Venice's 120 churches were flooded at the moment. Who was in charge of this disastrous desecration of holy spaces—God? Or Mother Nature? Or man? Whatever or whoever was to blame, it was a tragedy.

Is God in charge of weather events or is something else destroying towns and churches and wrecking people's lives? Does God control the weather, or are people alone making this happen? The existential thoughts occupied her mind for the moment. She never was very religious, but being in this sacred space was drawing it out of her.

Kora thought of herself as more spiritual than religious. Her higher-power connection was obviously to Mother Nature, but even with her superpowers, she could not fight back the forces of strong winds, flooding waters, superhurricanes, or fire. It seemed like God wasn't helping either in this crisis.

EcoQueen couldn't help but think about the other places that had been obliterated due to climate change in recent years: New Orleans; the Bahamas; Paradise, California. The list went on—whether from fire, hurricane, or sea level rise. The glimpse inside this sacred space was a sobering preview of how climate change, accelerated by human behavior, would not just complicate Venetians' unique and fragile way of life but wash it away entirely.

Feeling like she was starting to prune up from standing in water, despite her incredible suit, and wondering about what else from the city streets and canals was floating around her, EcoQueen questioned if there was even a way to reverse the devastating effects of global warming. Or was she fighting a lost cause?

In an attempt to help preserve the church at least, she blew hot air at the walls and the artwork to accelerate the rate at which it dried out. Like on the rare times she blow-dried her long black hair, she kept the blast of hot air moving. It was a windy mess in the basilica, but the save was huge.

The caretaker of the church appeared. He was in his sixties and loved the building intensely. His name was Vicente. He had no wife or children, having devoted his life to maintaining the basilica. Vicente considered those who congregated there his family, locals and tourists alike. In his lifetime, he carried the keys to the church—he was responsible for the physical well-being of the building that provided a spiritual home to so many. There had been generations of caretakers before him, and to all those stewards of the sacred space, it was not a job, it was a devotion. Some people found early on what it was they wanted to dedicate their life to, and Vicente was one of the lucky ones who found his calling.

He was short, bald on the top, and wore perfectly round spectacles, plus his waders, which were not working effectively since the water was up to his chest. He had seen acqua alta tides, and had experienced some flooding before, but like most other weather events that were occurring all over the globe, this one was what the news so commonly referred to now as *unprecedented*, a word that was getting worn out from repeated use these days.

When shock and loss and grief set in, it is hard to do anything or be productive in trying to make progress. He waded around the soggy church with his hand over his eyebrows, shaking his head in disbelief as if he could just shake off the trauma of it all. It was hitting his heart. This was a blow, as he felt history was being washed away in front of his eyes, and he knew only God could keep the water from rising, but for some reason, he wasn't.

He noticed EcoQueen, in the dark corner of the chapel, but he often saw ghosts in the church, so he was not struck by the movement and unexpected company.

The acqua alta siren sounded. Vicente listened intently. When he heard just one note, he said a little prayer of gratitude: the signal indicated that the next tide was predicted to rise only 110 centimeters above normal high tide. The city could handle that. He knelt down to fully genuflect and realized that the standing water in the basilica seemed to be receding, despite the still-rising tide. He didn't understand that this was EcoQueen's work, so he offered his thanks up to God. EcoQueen didn't mind at all.

CHAPTER 23

THE OCEANS ARE RISING AND SO ARE THE STUDENTS

CALIFORNIA

School finally opened again for students to attend in person. It had taken four full months to repair the electrical system of the building. They essentially had to rewire the whole school, carefully sewing new lines into already closed-off walls. It was technical and expensive, but they got it done. The students had been back in school for only a few hours, when suddenly, it seemed like the whole student body was flowing out of the building, walking the halls like salmon charging upriver. The energy was excited, engaged. Everyone—from freshmen to seniors—was walking out of the fourth period. It wasn't lunchtime, and it wasn't a passing period. They had just gotten up and walked out of class and were leaving the building, as an act of protest.

Apparently, this had been in the works for a month, and was organized over social media. Anyone who was online and a student at Tram High knew the plan for this student walkout after lunch, their first day back. Because, after all they had been through in their little community— the wildfire that was obviously a result of climate change—they couldn't return to school as if it were business as usual. The young people felt they needed to get involved for the sake of their future.

The Snapchat posts said, "Global Day of Climate Action! Come march with the millions of youth demanding climate action around the world," and "If you are a kid, you need to be part of this movement. Climate Action for Justice!" Every student who planned to grow up and live on the heating-up earth had a responsibility to do something now, for their own future. They needed to try and fix some things that were not working. They needed to speak out, to protest.

Some students were holding handmade signs written in Sharpie pens on deconstructed cardboard boxes. Others just looked excited to join in as a way to escape class, adding numbers to the march. The masses chanted, "The climate is changing, why aren't we?"

"What's going on? This doesn't seem like a fire drill!" Kora said to Bodi.

One kid held a sign over her head that said, "We Are Skipping Our Lessons to Teach You One!"

"This is the student climate rally. I'm sorry, did I forget to tell you about it? I thought we talked about it after you got back from Venice, but maybe you were just too tired. It's been all over Instagram, it's taking place all over the world today."

"Wow, this is fantastic, Bodi! A student walkout to demand change. Let's join in!"

Kora and Bodi slung their backpacks over their shoulders and slid into the flow of students streaming out of the building.

They smiled at each other and got swept up in the energy of a good old-fashioned peaceful protest. They marched with the four hundred or so other students to the soccer field, where a stage with a microphone and DJ table were set up. A girl with purple hair and a yellow jumpsuit was playing music that helped students march to the dance club beat toward the stage. It was festive. Students might get in trouble for walking out of class in a protest, but these students didn't care, as they knew that for their generation, the changing climate was way more important than detention. They jumped in and showed their solidarity and concern by being present and adding their bodies to the crowd.

They knew global warming was real, and they understood the urgency of the situation. To these students it felt like it had been all talk and no action for most of their lives, and now they were seeing the repercussions right there at home, affecting their lives: drought, fire, and sea level rise—oceans warming.

Kora was in complete accord. The words coming out of the reverberating PA speaker resonated deeply with her: "If you do nothing, nothing will happen. . . . If a fire started in your house, you would not sit back and do nothing, you would try to put it out! Fast. But as our planet burns, it feels like we are not doing enough to take action and put it out."

The organizer spoke enthusiastically into the microphone as students filed into the rally area. "Thank you for joining the other four million student activists who walked out of school today in the name of climate awareness. Kids like you and me are becoming victims of climate change in every country around the world. We have walked out to make it known, to the politicians and CEOs, to those who have the power to make decisions regarding our environment, to our teachers and our parents, that we have a crisis going on here and we need their leadership! We must listen to science!" The crowd roared in support and continued to grow.

Kora listened intently and said to Bodi, "It's so true!"

Inspired and empowered and clearly not shy to speak her mind, the twelfth-grade student at the mic was clear. "We must demand that leaders take climate action to protect *our* future. *Our* generation is scared and we need to take action. Thank you all for joining the fight!"

Bodi agreed, "It's so messed up. The other day there was a weird algae bloom at the beach. My surfing app kept giving me warnings about it. They were saying not to surf, to stay out of the water, that it was toxic. I heard that it's because the ocean temperature was so much warmer than usual, which encouraged the algae to bloom. I'd never seen anything like it before. The overgrowth of the algae and bacteria turned the ocean water red. It was freaky."

"Do you want to go to the beach and check it out? It's really weird?"

"Yeah, let's see how the waves look today. The app still says to stay out of the water."

"I think we are done at school here. In the name of climate change, let's go see what is happening to our poor ocean," Kora said. "A fitting end to a day of climate activism."

They jumped on their bikes and rode to their favorite beach. Kora and Bodi sat side by side on the warm sand and watched red waves fold in on themselves. What could they possibly do to help restore balance?

Bodi got his phone out to start reading some articles about the phenomenon aloud. Kora leaned even closer, trying to follow along. Suddenly, she felt woozy, and Bodi, the beach, and the sound of the pounding, apocalyptic surf faded away. . . .

***

Avalon took her seat on the air-conditioned shuttle and leaned her jet-lagged head against the window as the bus slowly inched down the congested highway from Beijing to Baoding, China. She could barely make out the rectangular shapes of the buildings that lined the highway as they were blurred by the thick haze and particulates in the air. She took off her sunglasses and gave them an instinctual rub on her cotton shirt, but that was not the issue. The sun had an Armageddon orange hue to it. She was one of the very few people coming into Baoding. Most people who had the resources were fleeing. There had already been one million smog refugees that were part of a mass exodus, which had left in search of breathable air. Her job was to make the air breathable again.

She took in a deep breath, but it made her cough. Her lungs weren't as ready as her brain for a new beginning. Tears pooled in her eyes, partly from the pollution, but to be honest, also from her heartbreak. Her stadium project was weeks away from completion. She felt like she was a different person now, but the pollution was the same or worse.

The Baoding stadium looked like a giant marshmallow from the outside. It was the former home to the national soccer team and had been used for track-and-field training. It was built by a famous Chinese architect who liked to make his stadiums resemble objects that usually could float in the sky. The exterior dome's original whiteness had been tarnished by the acid rain and soot in the air. It had been ideal for

Avalon's prototype to prove that cities could convert their stadiums into indoor rainforests and air-purifying machines.

Avalon and her team had set out to build an intricate reverse-filtration system that sucked in polluted air from outside, ran it through the rainforest closed-loop system, and delivered it back outside, with a synthetic algae added on to the respiring molecules that would then continue to eat the pollution when directed back into the outside environment.

When the building was a stadium it held 150,000 people in the bleachers, but, after Avalon's engineers, chemists, botanists, and physicists transformed it, it housed three hundred species of hard- and softwood rainforest trees that filtered the air through natural photosynthesis and respiration. The stadium forest was grown hydroponically and was the first biomimicry biodiverse forest grown without soil. The root system of the plant networks grew through the ceiling of the underground parking garage and hung from the rafters in the basement level, where a specialized team of horticulturists added the needed nutrients to the root ends each day to manipulate growth in the controlled environment.

When Avalon arrived at the project, her team greeted her. She had hired a group of international scientists that she was proud of. She was confident that they had continued to do great work on the project while she was back in Ecuador gathering the last data and specimens they needed.

On her first day back to the stadium project, she jumped right into her leadership role and marched around each level checking in, as if she had not been gone a day. With a notepad in hand, and her white coat back on, she was eager to receive their status reports.

"I've brought some more samples that I think will help in the filtration. Please get them transplanted as soon as possible," Avalon directed. An assistant softly embraced the specimens from her carry-on like a fragile firstborn baby and ran them down the hallway to get them in the hydroponic system with the organic biologist working in the main stadium.

"The rainforest is intact, healthy, and stable. We have just been waiting for you to turn on the filtration system. The engineers, programmers, chemists, and botanists have signed off on their parts. I am excited to say, it's ready to go," Lise, the head of the team she'd left behind, reported. "I think we may have done it, Avalon. I can't wait to see if your predictions are correct."

***

When Kora came to again, she was lying on her back in the warm sand. Bodi looked at her, concerned. "I hadn't realized you were so tired, Kora. Maybe we should go get something to eat? It's been a busy few days."

CHAPTER 24

CONGO MISSION

CONGO

They stayed to watch the big ball-of-fire sun set right over the ocean, due west, then rode their bikes slowly back to Bodi's trailer. Kora and Bodi threw together another round of smoothies with some old and bruised fruit sitting neglected and a bit sad looking in the crisper drawer in his fridge, plus some fruit from his freezer. Kora particularly loved inventing edible food creations from the dregs in the fridge. Bodi did most of the grocery shopping for himself and his mom. He did try to buy healthy food and not just junk, but also realized that fresh produce went bad quickly if you did not get on it and eat it in the first few days.

Kora needed to ask Bodi to push the Blend button on the machine when all the ingredients were there: coconut milk, apple juice, a bruised mango, wilted spinach, almond butter, some chocolate chips—and she tossed in the half-browning avocado at the end, just because. . . . It should be good enough. This one was going to be random and not taste impressive, but it was food, and they were hungry, and she was the master of the blender, as long as someone else pushed the button. She suspected that being so close to Bodi's phone had helped push her over the edge into the vision or dream she slipped into on the beach, and she wasn't ready for any more trippy visitations tonight. Best to stay far from anything plugged in or running on a battery.

Bodi checked the email on his computer as Kora poured "dinner" into cups. He blurted out in frustration, "Stuck again? It's a nonstop spinning beach ball on this thing. This computer is so old. . . . Wait, what? Kora, come check this out. Someone is trying to communicate with you through my computer."

Kora walked over in her flip-flops, with her hoodie sweatshirt pulled over her hair, and read the message from over Bodi's shoulder. It said: "EcoQueen, you are needed. For more details, type EQ now. Great job on your last mission BTW."

"Seriously? Now?" Kora said.

"Is that Río again? Are you going somewhere to save the earth?"

"It's my side hustle." She smirked at Bodi. Despite the fact that this meant there was a crisis endangering people somewhere, she had actually been craving the satisfaction of doing something powerful again. She was exhausted, but she realized that she was also quite excited to respond to the call to action.

"My superhero!" Bodi was intrigued, proud, and a little bit confused, but it was thrilling to see this side of his best friend.

"EcoQueen at your service! I've been around the block on a few missions. It's the most purposeful thing I have ever done in my life. The balance is clearly off. It's been one save after another, and it is not slowing down." Ponderings about her vision could wait. She was ready to check in with Río to see what the next climate disaster she would try to avert was. She had Bodi press the keys to initiate the video chat.

"Hi, Río. You remember my friend, Bodi? OK, bro, what do you have for me today?"

Río jumped right into the situation briefing. Fired up after the hundreds of hours of research he had done, he spouted out the memorized research facts. "The new 11,000-megawatt hydropower plant in the Democratic Republic of the Congo costs $14 billion. The Inga III dam is the biggest hydroelectric power station on Africa's second-longest river and provides much-needed electricity to the nation and others. Congo is one of the poorest countries in the world, but one of the richest in natural resources, and hydroelectric power could bring energy to villages that still do not enjoy this modern-day convenience . . . but it comes at the major expense of an entire ecosystem."

"So this is a man-versus-nature kind of thing?"

"A woman-versus-nature, superhero-versus-nature thing." He laughed and was proud of himself for making a little joke, even if the play on words didn't quite make sense to Kora.

"So, you want me to break down a dam?" Kora asked. "Because we should let the river do what it does, and flow without being tampered with?"

"Something like that. Ready?" Río was all set to activate teletransportation.

In order to switch gears from Kora to EcoQueen, Kora took a quick moment and a few breaths to get her body to align with the speed of her thoughts and the new information she was urgently bombarded with.

Kora turned to Bodi, who was standing next to her witnessing the preliminary communications. "Bodi, nobody knows about EcoQueen. So if my dad tries to reach me, could you be my cover?" He nodded, and she knew she could count on him. These days, her dad rarely checked in to see where she was or what she was up to anyway.

Kora and Bodi embraced in a longer-than-usual hug. They had never hugged like that before. It was a hug that said so many things in that touch: *be careful, be safe, don't get hurt, come back, I'll miss you,* maybe even *I love you in a way more than best friends. . . .*

Bodi gave her a quick kiss on the cheek, and said, "I'll always have your back." That was their special bond. They had an understanding that they would do whatever it was for each other to help make the normal suffering of life a little easier if they could. That was true friendship, or maybe even something a little bit more? Deeply and truly, they both just wanted to be each other's person in the best way they knew how.

She waved to Bodi and put her fingers on the keys of the computer, pushed Control + E + Q, and got sucked into the computer again, diving in headfirst, like she did to each hard thing.

Bodi saw her vanish into the screen this time, but was assured that she would be back. He knocked on the screen. Unfortunately, it did not grasp him, too. He wondered what was behind the teletransport. He had heard about this potential technology, but couldn't believe his own friend Kora was one of the first people to get to use it.

***

Kora was getting accustomed to teletransport, much like a fireman and the pole, on her way to rescue. This time, she relaxed into it. Knowing that she was going for a ride, she was able to focus her energies to avoid setting fire to the computer and Bodi's house. She relinquished the urge to fight it, grabbed onto the fiber-optic cables, and held on for the wild ride.

EcoQueen came flying out of a different computer screen, forcefully ejected from a desktop computer in the control tower of the Inga III hydroelectric power station on the Congo River. The control center for the dam was constructed from industrial steel, concrete, and glass. The room was crisp and air-conditioned, even though the outside air temperature of the valley was Africa-hot—unbearable and oppressive.

EcoQueen looked out the floor-to-ceiling glass windows and saw a hazed-out red African sun and a crispy dried landscape on the edges of the flood caused by the controlled water of the dam project. She saw mostly engineered concrete and high gray walls all around. What had once been land on the riverbanks was now river bottom. The Congo River used to enjoy a regular rainy season, collecting precipitation from rain patterns from both above and below the equator. But in the last several years, with manipulation of the river for use in new dams like this, the weather patterns had changed. Mess with nature, and everything gets out of balance. Less than three of the average thirty-four inches of rain fell from the sky in the last few years, which resulted in drought, failed crops, hunger, and instability.

EcoQueen took a moment to contemplate and knew she needed to make a crucial decision: total biodiversity destruction and progress in the form of electricity for all, or ecosystem recovery and forcing the hands of those who had the power to help develop new, more environmentally friendly technologies. Hydroelectric power, in itself, was not fossil fuel energy, so that was good, but at the same time, in this situation, there were many harmful repercussions. It was a familiar debate: Should man alter nature in the name of progress? Or should man, and woman, try to restore nature at this point? EcoQueen's decision was made.

She walked out on top of the massive concrete wall, ten feet thick and six hundred feet high, constructed to hold back the potential energy of Inga Falls and capture its power in turbines. This hydropower plant was the largest in the world, producing twice as much energy as the Three Gorges dam in China, bigger even than the Itaipú dam between Brazil and Paraguay. The Inga hydropower plant was hailed as the Holy Grail for power, harnessing sub-Saharan Africa's most magnificent river. It could light up half of the continent that had largely been left in the dark after the industrial revolution, many of its nations still developing their energy infrastructure.

The mist came up from the crashing water being diverted through the intake channels of the dam and out through the turbine. Obviously, when a river was dammed, the water flow diminished, the river became shallower, and the sun warmed the water to higher temperatures. Fish could no longer spawn and sedimentation became a problem, but there was still a massive amount of water in the reservoir to use. EcoQueen felt that her plan could ultimately help the millions of people who were struggling with lack of water, not to mention millions of fish, bird, and animal species that lived in that area of Congo.

She saw the value of bringing hydroelectricity to homes across Central Africa, especially when it empowered children to read and study at night to get educated. But she also knew the withheld water was needed in other ways: to drink, to grow food, to water the dehydrated soils of the land. Water is life. EcoQueen was aware of that.

She needed to take drastic action to force people to invest more in the alternative forms of power that weren't destroying the ecosystem. It was possible to have both electrical power and a healthy world. The technology already existed, but EcoQueen needed to make the unhealthy, shortsighted choices less convenient.

Her solution was going to require a complicated move that she needed to execute with precision in midair while she was falling. There was no room for error, even though she had never jumped from that height before. She had one chance as she took the six-hundred-foot jump from the top of the dam wall. As a superhero, she did not fly, even though at this moment she really wished that she did. Maybe she'd ask Río to work on some jets for her suit or something. But what she did have, literally at her fingertips, was her power and energy, and she had to use them now.

She placed her heels on the edge of the dam wall to set herself up like an Olympic high diver preparing for a backflip off the board. With a bend in her knees and the swing of her arms, she pushed off backward from her heels and began a free fall facing the wall. As if she had gathered the extra kinetic energy from the falling water, her exhale focused her strength from her centerline. She fired focused power, like laser beams, out from her eyes, forehead, mouth, fingers, and even belly button, as she fell, etching a burn line that looked like a zipper into the concrete from top to bottom. The crack was black and faint. And then, finally, EcoQueen splashed into the water below.

She was immediately pulled downstream in the fast currents at the base where the turbines spit out water, generating three million horsepower. Using all her might, she attempted to swim back upstream. With each freestyle stroke of her arms, she eked out a few more blasts toward the bottom part of the wall that held the immense pressure of water behind it. A hairline fracture down the million tons of concrete in the dam wall created a big enough trickly leak that water started to flow back into the river. One hand at a time, she directed the lightning energy from her fingers toward the dam, as she swung them overhead to dig each stroke into the water. The currents pulled her farther down the river, but the laser beams still hit the wall even though her distance increased.

Like strips of Velcro no longer strong enough to hold on to the other side, the hairline fracture cracked. The concrete dam ruptured in a significant break, where excess water flowed through—escaping, but not flooding. And it did what water does, and flowed downhill with gravity, with elation, as if just released from jail. Concrete chunks shattered and were sprinkled into the river below. The wall of water jumped the banks and spilled over, doubling the path of the river that had been diminished to barely a stream. EcoQueen faced her feet downstream and readied herself for the ride of a lifetime, as she was now part of the currents she created.

She grabbed a piece of wooden debris from the water, planted her soles on it, got up, and surfed it. With her shoulder guiding her planted back foot, EcoQueen carved turns to steer the river to spots that had not seen water since the dam was built. The river went from a pathetic trickle back to a real flow. All the way down, she helped distribute the water to places that needed it most. The river knew where to go because it had once lived there before it was held back.

Well, it looks like I have no choice but to take a river trip. I guess I will just have to go with the flow here. She laughed at her own stupid pun.

She got to the bank and pulled herself up onto the rocky shore a mile downstream from the damaged dam wall that was still spilling water. She made a few modifications on her board, trimming it down and carving it with some precision heating from her fingertips to form a practical design, with an artistic touch, and shaped a smooth, sleek, and sturdy board she could stand up on and paddle. Once complete, she ran her hands over it to admire the form, and then she jumped on it.

The river had gone from rapids to a more relaxed flow. Its churning turquoise waters began to slow and move without ripple as one big body of water. She wondered what the river basin had looked like before the stream was reconstructed with a different plan for it, altered and controlled. She knew from learning about other massive dam projects that populations who originally lived along the shores of the river and depended on it for their livelihood were displaced and forced to move when the intentional flooding occurred.

As EcoQueen paddled, she thought about how whenever humanity gets in the way of nature, there is always some kind of environmental backlash. The first few strokes on the stand-up paddleboard felt like she was floating over a graveyard—EcoQueen knew that creatures had drowned under there when she restored the river's natural path. She was sad, but she understood that it was best for all life when the river could decide for itself where it would go.

Power is what makes the world go round these days, she thought and wondered if the planet was at the point of no return. She had once read that if the atmosphere had more than 350 particulates of carbon dioxide per million, it would be the tipping point where the atmosphere would not be able to reverse the warming. She wondered what it was now.

Río's audio came in through her hood, which was helping to block the pounding sun off her face. Having read her last thought, through the wiring in the hood and their special twin connection, he inter-jected himself into her serene float, when she thought she was all alone.

"CO_2 in the atmosphere just exceeded 415 parts per million for the first time in human history." He was excited to be able to report to her, there on the Congo River. She digested that information, and realized sometimes knowing was worse than not knowing.

"Thanks for the data, Río." At least it was reassuring to be reminded that she wasn't all alone out there.

Could she, or the people of the world, actually do anything to turn this climate crisis around? She thought a lot about the role she put herself in. Taking action and being of service definitely made her feel like she had a purpose. Actually, doing something helped her mood after all that had happened. But she also felt like the global warming problem was way too big for one superhero to address on her own, and she questioned if she was actually helping long-term or just putting a Band-Aid on the problems. At times the challenges felt too monumen-tal and the behavior driving it too entrenched: massive storms, rising oceans alongside droughts, slash-and-burn logging operations, new oil drilling, coal power plants continuing to be built.

As she drifted on the new lazy current of the river, being solo in nature, she managed her thoughts and reflected. She was grateful for this time, this moment. One of her coping mechanisms when grief threatened to overwhelm her was to list all that she was grateful for in her life. That usually worked as a way to fend off depression and bore-dom. It felt good to be going slowly and not running around putting out fires, so to speak.

She remembered advice from Ms. Piper: "When in doubt, always have hope." If she let all her globe-trotting to devastated areas for disaster relief burn her out, she wouldn't be able to feel that in the big picture she was really helping solve the most serious problems.

What would be the next climate emergency? How could she possi-bly find the energy for resolving whatever climate issue decided to rear its head next? Could it possibly get any worse? Her instinct was yes. It wasn't a matter of how but when would she have to respond.

As EcoQueen drifted, she wondered if people would ever start making decisions to preserve and conserve the land instead of profit from it. That was how the indigenous people had lived harmoniously on the land for all this time. But they were getting squeezed out, fast, over a greater desire for drilling, logging, and extracting from the earth instead of protecting it.

As she paddled down the river, she saw some human activity around the bend up ahead. It had been pretty remote, just her and nature the whole ride so far. But up ahead, about one hundred people busily moving, carrying things, and digging next to the river looked like a colony of worker ants. She realized that until now, she hadn't seen a soul since her mission started.

The people were busy with shovels and buckets and pickaxes. As the workers came into better focus, she realized that many of them were young kids around the age of thirteen or fifteen, not many even as old as she was. Some wore rubber boots while others were in flip-flops, but all were dressed in stained tank tops and soggy muddied half-legged pants. These school-age kids looked like they'd never had the luxury of school, but instead they spent their days sifting minerals out of the mud.

This was a tedious and outdated way to mine, much like how the gold miners in California panned in riverbeds back in the nineteenth century. The children knelt in muddy craters that they dug by hand in the fertile mineral lands of the streambed, scraping away dirt to find the small pebble-size nugget of a common metallic type of stone that the world depended on, yet their pay never added up to enough to eat well for that day or the next. Taking precious minerals out from the earth to be used for human progress was backward in itself, as it also caused much destruction.

The Democratic Republic of the Congo had some of the most precious natural resources in the world, with fertile soils that swelled with abundant deposits of copper, gold, and uranium, too. These natural resources would make you think this might be one of the world's wealthiest countries. But actually, Congo was one of the most impoverished places in the world.

Río had EcoQueen on satellite drone video and was watching her every move to assure her safety. Confident from mission control from his own desktop computer, Río typed in her exact location and identified the mine. He quickly researched it to understand what was going on there. He read aloud to her:

"Columbite-tantalite, also known as coltan, an ore from which niobium and tantalum are extracted, is mined here. As a stone, it looks a bit like a chunk of coal, black and a bit metallic. Coltan is one of the most critical minerals that make the modern world go round. Civilization can no longer live without it. Coltan is used to construct electronic capacitors, a fundamental component of cell phones and other electronics. Tantalum is the critical mineral ingredient responsible for the miniaturization of handheld electronic devices, as it allows electricity to be stored in a small capacitor. In other words, coltan is a crucial component of modern life. It is in every electronic device in use today." As he read out loud to his sister, it also helped him process the information himself.

Río used lots of devices all day long because he loved them, and when he thought about it, he was surrounded by coltan in every direction he looked: on the four desktop screens on his corner desk, his two cell phones, three iPads, and even on his 3D printer. They made his life what it was. It was that connection with the world, and his sharing of his mind, that made him feel complete.

Curious, ready for a break, and excited to see people, EcoQueen paddled near the muddy riverside operation. She jumped off her board and placed both feet firmly on the ground, but it still felt like she was floating on water with sea legs under her. Her head started to spin; she noticed her heartbeat rising, too. A drop of sweat slipped down her face, and her breaths shortened. She took a few big gulps of oxygen, but still felt odd. She thought to herself, *Good thing I got off the river, I didn't know I was seasick until I stopped.*

The kids looked up at her, surprised by this young woman in her superhero costume, boots, belt, armbands, bracelet, and all, stepping off a paddleboard into their mining operation. A child named Soli, who was working at the mine, smiled at her and waved, excited to see something different in his long twelve-hour day sifting ore from the dirty pools under the hot African sun. The other young workers knew not to stop, although they did wish for a break, too. Most were too terrified even to look EcoQueen's way, knowing their bosses were watching their every move, with machine guns in hand. But little Soli, inherently kind and curious, approached with his broad smile, sporting a healthy space between his recently grown-in adult front teeth.

"Hello, ma'am. What are you doing here?" His cute voice was excited. He loved new people, and his mom had always taught him to greet with a smile, so he did.

"I'm taking a break from being on the river," Kora said. "Is it OK if I stop here for a second? I'm suddenly not feeling so good." She managed to get the words out, though her speech slowed and she began to slur.

EcoQueen started to experience a splitting headache, and after taking only a few steps inland toward the sweet boy, she felt dizzy and lost her balance. She sat down on the bank, wondering what had suddenly come over her, when she had been fine a few minutes back. She slumped and put her head between her legs.

"Are you OK, ma'am?" Soli asked EcoQueen, as it looked like she was about to drift off for a nap in a strange place.

"I'm just feeling a little queasy. I guess I have been on the paddleboard too long." She paused and looked around at the miners. "What kind of operation is this?" She bent over and picked up an apricot-pit-size rock from the pile of black rocks that looked dull but shimmered in the sun.

Suddenly, EcoQueen's arms and legs started to shake furiously. She tried to control it, but she couldn't. She was having a seizure—something that had never happened to her before. Her eyes rolled back, and she started sweating profusely—her hands clenched, her jaw did, too, and she started foaming from her lips, and then she went limp right there on the shore, spread out on the ground.

Río saw this briefly from his satellite imaging, but then his screen went dark, just like his sister's world at the moment.

Soli did not know what to do. He called his boss with the machine gun who had been facing the other way, monitoring another group of young miners, and yelled for him to come over. The guard was older, all of twenty-one years old, and Soli thought he would know what to do with this stranger in a cape, who just showed up and passed out on their mining site. Soli fanned her face and reached for her arm to get a pulse like he had seen his mom do to the sick people who would come to their hut for care.

Río tried desperately to reboot and realign his satellite, his video camera, his signal. He was in a bit of a panic, trying to see what happened to his equipment or the connection. He realized the power in his house was out. No Wi-Fi, no lights, and definitely no teletransport rescue. EcoQueen was stranded in Congo.

"Sir, this lady has fainted!" Soli told the guard. "What should we do?"

The guard, startled to see a strange face at their illegal mining site, said, "Who is she and where did she come from?" His worry was more about foreign surveillance taking note of the work they were doing than the well-being of this random teenage girl.

Soli shrugged.

A few of the adult guards hurried around in the chaos to get a closer look. They did not get the feeling that this girl had come to the mine to rob it or expose it. They didn't know why she was there or who she was with, but it looked like she was dying on them. This, they certainly did not want to happen on their watch. Maybe she was an investigative journalist who was going to report on the poor conditions of the mine or the exploitation of the children workers or the environmental destruction they were creating. Whatever it was, they knew they had to get her out of there and get her some help before word got back to whatever group she was with that she had died.

"Is she breathing?" one child laborer asked.

Soli checked to see if he could feel breath on his cheek and listened for any life. "Slow, shallow, but she is still alive. What should we do?"

"Shake her! Slap her face. I have seen my auntie do this to my uncle when he is sleeping in the alley," another kid suggested.

Soli knew this was not a drunken faint; it was something else, but he didn't know what. He called out, "This girl needs help! We can bring her to my mother. She is a healer. She will know what to do."

Finally the main mine boss, more adult than any of the workers or guards, came to the scene with his AK-47 slung over his right shoulder. He pushed everyone out of the way to get to EcoQueen. He gathered her limp and light body up in his arms, all 111 pounds of her, and said, "Come, Soli. We will bring her to your mother."

After he scooped her up, he put her in the Jeep. Soli jumped in the back seat so he could hold her head on his lap, as her body slumped like dead weight into the torn-up upholstery. They sped off along the extremely rutted dirt road back to the camp where Soli lived, the boy protecting her as much as he could.

CHAPTER 25

GLOBAL SHUTDOWN

CONGO

Soli's house was a piece of tin for a roof and three makeshift walls. His mother was a tall and slender Congolese woman with her hair cut short like her son's. She saw the Jeep come in and wondered if there had been an accident. Soli usually walked back from the mine and arrived right before dusk, but it was midday.

The Jeep pulled right up to where she was cooking over a small open fire in the back of their shanty house. The mine guards were stone-faced and not in a hurry to explain the situation of the stranger they had with them. They tried to keep their presence intimidating there at the camp, moving deliberately to show that they were in control.

Everyone there knew that the high price tag on the minuscule shards of coltan they found was money used to fund the ongoing war with neighboring Rwanda, so it was best left undiscussed. And it was best if outsiders stayed out. They surely did not want the rest of the world to know, especially Apple and Samsung, who were their biggest clients for the conflict-laden coltan. Apple alone sold 849,450 iPhones a day worldwide; more than nine iPhones sold per second. Soli made five dollars a day in comparison. Coltan was big money for others, but not for the people living in this camp. Still, it could mean the difference between a full cooking pot and an empty one.

They rolled EcoQueen out of the back seat like a noodle. Her normally taupe-colored skin was ash gray. She was motionless, and they delivered her like a sack of potatoes to the hut. Soli jumped out of the Jeep and hugged his mom. The guards climbed back in the Jeep and raced away, glad to be rid of this inconvenience.

"This lady, she showed up at the mine today, and then passed out. She is sick—can you help her, Mama?" Soli asked. He was genuinely concerned, as he always was for any living being. Soli bowed down with a feeling of humility toward all of existence and felt like everything was a part of him, not separate.

Soli's mom was a fifth-generation healer and one of the only medical helpers around the camp. She often tended to the miners, the mothers, and the children when anyone was in need, sick, or having an emergency. Armed with wisdom from her mom and her grandmother before her, Soli's mom, Delanda, never had any formal schooling, but people were always bringing her sick patients. Most of the time, she was able to help them with the knowledge of herbs, mushrooms, and healing touch that had been passed on to her from her family line. She had been teaching Soli, too, which might have been why he was so compassionate at the scene of EcoQueen's seizure.

Río, in the meantime, was beyond stressed, sensing something was hugely wrong, larger than just the blackout. His computer was dead, but was his sister, too? There was no way for him to make the connection because all the power was out—inside her as well. He no longer could see her GPS location or get her vitals from her suit. All his intel was down, and he felt beyond helpless. He no longer had a feed on her safety, whereabouts, or health. He wasn't even getting any of his twin-sense feedback.

In his worry, Río began to panic and hit buttons on his desktop to reset, reboot, refresh. But nothing worked. The connection was cut. He noticed the fan in his living room had stopped spinning, too. It was as if everything was holding its breath. The power was out. Little did he know, at that moment, it was out all over the world as well.

Meanwhile, back in Africa, Delanda, the calm healer, said, "Bring her in, Soli. Here. We'll do it together."

Soli and his mom carried EcoQueen into the hut and gently laid her on the handwoven carpet that covered the earth floor.

Delanda said, "Young lady, where in the world did you come from? You are clearly not from here. But, hang on, because I can help you." She could already sense EcoQueen had some kind of advanced energy in her, and that she seemed to have short-circuited. Delanda just had to figure out how to jump-start this superhero, who was now so vulnerable.

EcoQueen had a pulse, and her chest was rising; she was still alive, but the lights were out. Delanda scanned her body to try and make an assessment. She passed her intuitive hands above EcoQueen's still body, asking for guidance in the diagnosis. *Was it a snakebite? Something poisonous? Heatstroke? An allergic reaction?* Those possibilities didn't feel likely, but she got a sense that something was off in the girl's otherwise healthy system.

Delanda worked some herbs into a smooth paste that she applied to EcoQueen's forehead to help reduce her fever. She painted on a liquid with a pungent smell under her nose in an attempt to rouse her. She lit some candles and spoon-fed EcoQueen a special broth, pooling it in her cheek with hopes that it would absorb. It was night now, and after Delanda exhausted all the medicine she could scrounge in her healing kitchen, she proceeded to pray over the innocent stranger in her hut, for her to become well again. She stroked her hair, cooled her brow with a cloth, and brushed it over her cheekbones, throat, heart, and belly button. Delanda wanted to see her get well; nothing filled her heart like healing others.

EcoQueen's hands were still clenched and rigid like rigor mortis. Thinking that she would try to stimulate the reflexology points in her hands, Delanda uncurled EcoQueen's clenched fists, only to find she was holding on to a solid rock of coltan.

EcoQueen's contact with the coltan must have caused an electrical surge the size of a solar flare that disrupted the electrons not just in her system, but globally. Somehow, EcoQueen's power in proximity to raw coltan disrupted circuitry worldwide. A force of electrical powers combined with the minerals caused the earth to go dark and off-line. The coltan was clearly EcoQueen's kryptonite, and the two together caused a problem even more enormous and urgent than global warming: a global power outage.

The balance was lost, and the delicate system, which most of humanity now relied on, scrolled back to how it had been two hundred years ago, before AC/DC electrical power through power lines existed. Since August 6, 1991, the day the World Wide Web became available to the public, 4.4 billion people relied on it minute to minute. For many of the seven billion people who lived on earth, the connection to this online world, charged by electricity alone, became essential for survival. Big data and information stored in the cloud managed everything from a local diner's ordering system to the global economy's stock trading. Going without it was almost undoable. Most people born after the year 2000 hadn't spent a day in their life without the internet, forgetting to be grateful for the information superhighway that worked for them around the clock and rarely ever shut off. It had never blacked out like this since its inception.

The interconnected power grid that humankind had grown to rely on in the present day had been disrupted. As Río's screen went dark, so did those of every other person on the planet. The electrical power of the world had been cut off. Progress stopped. And the world did not know how to deal without the ever-present, all-important data connection.

It happened abruptly, from "game on" to "all off." Like it came as an order from the gods, of the higher power . . . Everyone had somehow jumped on the treadmill and didn't realize what life could be like if they jumped off. It was a force quit on a global level. Control, Alt, Delete . . . Was this the reboot of modern civilization or the crash?

The short circuit created a significant pause. The incident made people momentarily realize that everything was not OK, and most people had not been paying attention until now. The earth was catching fire, and yet, business as usual had not made it stop. The glaciers were melting, but nobody was making the change to prevent it. The earth, the soil, the air, the water were all polluted, but was anything being done about it? The earth was at the point of the sixth extinction.

A polar bear crying on the last piece of ice, but nobody could hear it. Forests were getting slashed and burned, but most people turned their heads. It was hard to listen if you were so busy, climbing higher and higher. What were people climbing for?

The earth itself seemed to be asking humanity to reassess: *This will help. It will hurt. Take a deep look at what you are doing and how you are living and consuming—food, water, fuel, waste. Why run around and neglect your own family and your own health? Stop, and take a moment: How are you doing? How is your home and how is your health? Look at the sky, how is it doing? Look at the ocean and rivers, how are they? Look at yourself. You can't be well!*

Like EcoQueen, who lay there with all the life drained out of her.

At first, people thought the blackout must have been an isolated outage affecting their neighborhood or town or city. Global knowledge of the event was slow to spread, because there was no communication across states or countries or continents in order to learn it was happening simultaneously everywhere power existed. That wasn't figured out until days later.

Entire computer networks crashed. Banking halted, commerce stopped, navigation was interrupted—trade, business, flights all stalled.

In Jacksonville, Florida, a man walked up to an ATM. Power was out, money couldn't be accessed, all banking was frozen. A woman with a child went to a small market in New York City, but could not buy her groceries because the credit card reader would not register. The food in the café in Istanbul was no longer chilling, and soon it would need to be tossed, as the hot outside air was causing it to spoil without refrigeration. A delivery truck driving through Vancouver, BC, no longer had its GPS and the driver did not know where and what she was delivering, not to mention the traffic lights were not working, making mayhem on the roads. A man in Montana was miles from home and out of gas, but the pump at the station would not work without power from the grid. A patient on the operating table in London, England, in the middle of open-heart surgery, would not survive if the machine keeping his heart beating stopped pumping for him.

Nobody knew how long this would go on, and if they should brace for survival mode as the minutes turned to hours. They worried if it would be days or weeks this way. The world was a ball of tension, but still in session, and wondering how the blackout would unfold. The power freeze was in play, and the present moment of turned-off screens was dropping the planet into another space. The reactions were fierce and mesmerizing. Depending on the makeup of the user, the reaction was to reconnect off-line or to come undone. It was a brand-new engagement with life, without screens.

Delanda unraveled EcoQueen's fingers and the small chunk of coltan fell from her grip. The little piece of coltan dropped and rolled until it came to a stop on the earthen floor of Delanda's hut. Delanda and Soli stared at the black rock sitting motionless, and both registered the life changer that it was. They gazed at it, on the same wavelength of the known possibilities, but said nothing. That rock could change their world.

Usually, the armed guards hovered around the miners to make sure nobody was sneaking even a speck of the coltan into their boot when leaving the mine. They made all the workers empty their pockets each day before they left the mine to assure that nobody was stealing their profits. When Soli realized EcoQueen had smuggled out this precious metal, he thought about all the possibilities that could open up for him and his mom if they were to cash that rock in on the black market for an opportunity elsewhere. The piece of coltan could get them out of the horrible poverty they were living in at the labor camp; it could buy them food, shelter, health, opportunity. It was a ticket out of this life and into a better one—a small black rock held so much value. Was this stealing? Or was it making good on a lousy situation? They were elated and scared at the same time because of the rock that was now in their hut. Soli gracefully picked up the mineral, wrapped it in a dirty sock, put it in an empty tin can. He and his mother brought it outside the shanty and hid it under their cook pot in the ashes of the fire from breakfast.

At that moment, EcoQueen miraculously started to come back to life.

When Delanda came back into the hut, she was delighted to see EcoQueen sitting up, eyes open, and her hand instinctively pulling back her hair.

"Oh, child, you came back to us!"

"Where am I? What just happened?" EcoQueen asked, having just woken from unconsciousness, too weak to even try and put all the pieces together. She only wanted to rest but could feel blood rushing and circulating again.

At the very moment when the coltan rock was dislodged from EcoQueen's hand, the global blackout was resolved. The lights flickered back on in the White House alarm system, and the ventilation system started pumping again in the Louvre in Paris. Buckingham Palace, which had once been lit with flames but now was fully wired, was illuminated again. The airports and runways lit back up to guide planes in for landing, and the control towers and communications were up and running again. People's internet connections lit up to five great arching bars on laptops in Singapore, iPhones in India, smartphones in Brazil—happy, buzzing, busy, and lit.

Humanity rejoiced because they all felt how bad it could have been if this crisis had gone on any longer. Simultaneously, they realized their dependence on energy to keep things normal. The world went from offline to online again, a full global reboot. Fear and anxiety subsided as humanity settled back into business as usual. But a global power outage that long had never happened before. As they say, you don't know what you got 'til it's gone.

Mysteriously, when the screens came back on, and all the computers around the world were refreshed, the same message appeared for everyone, on every screen, in languages tied to the geography of the grid.

"Global Warming Emergency. Time to Wake Up!"

This message appeared on all devices connected to the internet that fired up after the blackout. It planted a seed of an idea in everyone who had been feeling the effects of the blackout: how they would react to the situation was critical. Control + Z, reset, was in order.

The message appeared on Nelson's computer in the hills of South Africa, where he sat at his desk secretly waiting for the superhero to return, enjoying a fresh cup of water from a glass.

Kora's dad read the worldwide message "Global Warming Emergency. Time to Wake Up!" but quickly tried to get to his work email, a screen of more importance to him. The lights of the message reflected off his eyes, blinking red in bold letters, almost stubbornly. That made him think about his fights with Kora about global warming, and he wondered if she had gotten the hacked message, too, and if it had made her happy. Then he celebrated when he was able to get back online to check in on the status of his most important work project.

Most people around the world stopped and wondered for a moment what this message was supposed to mean. Who was sending it? *Strange*, they thought, but it was a message that they obviously needed to heed. Before this public service announcement revealed itself to the world, it never felt like global warming was a common problem. After the universal blackout, this message made it clearer that it was a worldwide effort, and everyone needed to get on board in some way or another.

Small actions, as well as monumental actions, all counted. The message to the world went out, and everyone who enjoyed access to the internet—4.4 billion people on earth out of the 7 billion—read the message at the same time.

Rosa read it in Ecuador, her phone vibrating and alerting her as it came back to life. She knew exactly what it meant; her indigenous people had always recognized the importance of keeping the earth in balance.

Río saw the message from his laptop in Australia and was pleased with how it turned out. Not surprisingly, he had worried about this scenario—that global connection could be knocked out for a long time due to a massive climate event. It actually kept him up at night. So, two years before this global pause ended up happening, he had proactively programmed a message to the world for when the internet was restored.

Río was well aware that every single person in the world got the wake-up call that he had orchestrated. He was also relieved to be back online. He needed to track down his sister so he could help get EcoQueen back to safety.

Using the satellite connection that finally came online again, Río used those channels of digital communication to get her out of there. He had recently made this advancement to his original teletransport fiber-optic travel. He was proud that it now worked through satellite signals, and he could use that in this remote situation, where the internet connection was sparse. If there was a will, there was a way. Now that the power was back up, an internet connection was possible to any corner of the globe. So many things felt possible! And Río was on it.

CHAPTER 26

IS DAD THE VILLAIN?

CALIFORNIA

When Kora got home, it felt like so much had changed in the world, but still there was so much work to be done—in climate change crises as EcoQueen, but also as a concerned member of her community. She was inspired by the activism and action she saw around her from classmates and neighbors, but more needed to be done to help bring the world back from the brink of environmental disaster.

To Kora, it felt like there was no middle ground around climate science. Some people absolutely denied the problems. Opinions were intense and partisan, even in high school. She heard this had a lot to do with social media, and what each person was being fed as far as information. She tried the experiment that she heard about in a documentary, asking Bodi to start to type into Google "climate change is . . ." to see what autofill gave him for choices, based on his data search history. He got "climate change is caused by," "climate change is not a hoax," "climate change is real," and "climate change is it too late." Kora had Bodi type a search into her dad's tablet. Duncan was professionally deeply connected to the fossil fuel industry, with a very different viewpoint and search history than Bodi. Her dad's autofill suggestions were all skeptical: "Climate change is . . . controversial," "lacks scientific evidence," "is behind manufacturing uncertainty."

It could be hard for some people to know what to believe anymore, even after a global event like the blackout. You might think that an engineer like Duncan would follow the facts, but his bank account held too much sway. This made the gap between Kora and her dad even more monumental, a divide as deep as the Grand Canyon, where she stood on one side believing one thing about the climate, and he was on the other with his opinion. In this day and age, it seemed like nobody knew how to meet in the middle and respectfully agree to disagree, even father and daughter.

Kora felt deep down in her bones that it was humans' responsibility to help keep nature in balance. She was passionate about conservation and treading lightly on the earth. Duncan was the type of man who needed the natural resources of the earth to make progress as humans. And so they faced off, like boxers do, coming at each other from their different corners to see who was stronger and would win the fight.

Now that he was an unwilling single dad, and Blythe was not around him anymore with her little acts of greenness, Duncan found no need, time, or energy to be the environmental good guy. He never refused the straw, brought his own coffee cup to refill, or carried his own cloth grocery bags into the market. He gave up on those little things that he felt were just feel-good actions and really made no greater impact on the earth as a whole. Who cared whether he got his beer can in the recycling bin or not? He needed to be saved more than the earth. He sensed that his grief had pushed him to the verge of diving into the deep end on the mental health front. He couldn't be bothered with one more external stressor or effort, because taking care of himself with the depression, exhaustion, stress, and grief he had to fight off every day in an attempt to stay normal was overwhelming him.

Kora's mom had been a recycling stickler, and would actually dig through the garbage can to remove a #2 plastic yogurt container in order to get it safely on its journey into the recycling bin and beyond. She was the one who insisted on LED lights and low-flow toilets for their house and supported Kora in the outdoor compost pile they built together in the backyard, where they transformed their food waste into regenerative soil.

Blythe had been a bridge between Kora and her generation and the apathetic older generation who were so conditioned to a disposable lifestyle that they created more than their body weight in waste every day and weren't even aware of it.

The night after Kora came back from Congo and the world received Río's wake-up call, Kora's dad walked into their disheveled hotel room, his eyes red from too many hours staring into the screen. The lost hours of the blackout had caused a backlog of emergencies at his work.

He rarely ever left his work behind. It followed him, in his head, wherever he went, and he had gotten to the point where as long as he could bury himself in his software projects, he didn't have to deal with the other emotions that he was trying so hard to stuff down into a place where they couldn't bother him.

Kora had been sitting in the living room. Her experiences in Congo had given her a strong sense of her own mortality. Her dad was her family, and she couldn't bear to think that he wouldn't have cared if she never came back, or that he still didn't care that every day at work, he made the world less viable for her future. She wanted to talk with him to ask what he'd thought about Río's message.

"Kora, I'm flying to Russia for an urgent meeting. You'll be OK here on your own for the week, right? I'll leave you money for food. You can order DoorDash every day if you want, I don't care. Use my account. . . . Oh right, you don't use a phone. I'll leave you some cash."

At one point, Kora had realized that Duncan had set a reminder in his phone that came up at 6:00 p.m. every day—"Feed Kora"—as if she were the house pet or something.

Duncan opened his wallet and handed Kora some cash. Kora glanced at the many paper dollar bills in her hand. She folded the dirty bills into a small origami rectangle and stuck it in the front pocket of her jeans. Kora acknowledged her dad with an empty "Thank you," and he returned to his room.

Sad that this was the only form of love she got from him, at the same time Kora realized that the money he just handed her could feed a village in Guatemala for a month. She considered turning around and donating it all. To her, money was something like breath—it goes in and goes out—and this, she was highly aware, was part of the privilege she was adopted into. She couldn't help but wonder, every time she was passed a twenty-dollar bill by her parents, what that much money might have felt like to her if she were growing up in the Amazon in Ecuador.

One thing she knew for certain, that she had seen in her neighborhood and even in her own home, was that more money didn't bring more happiness. This knowledge she kept front and center, to try to ensure she never got really attached to dollars. At least this little chunk of money that her dad made from the fossil fuel industry could be passed through and redirected to a cause she felt passionate about. She'd spend some at her favorite vegan food truck, she'd spend some at the organic food co-op, and she'd hand the rest to the older woman on the street with a cardboard sign that said, "Lost Everything in the Fire."

Kora craved more care from her dad but also knew that he might not be capable of this while he was in mourning. Duncan always seemed like he was in motion, moving and talking while doing, leaving and reappearing, eating while in transit, on his phone while driving, walking or pacing. He never really paused entirely to be and breathe. It was as if he was always running, not letting reality catch up with him, to avoid just being and absorbing what was.

She wondered what had happened to him while she was away, in the coma in Congo, when the world had shut down around him. She wished she could talk to somebody about what happened to her, and she also craved to know what kind of impact the global pause had had on her dad and everyone else. Did it change them or make them think? Were those just more scrolling words? Did it plant a seed of change or ideas for anyone?

"What are you doing in Russia, Dad?" she asked as she moved toward his bedroom. She stopped in the hallway outside his room, not wanting to actually go in and enter into his space.

"I'm getting a new plant up and running with my software. The global blackout set us back on remote training, so I need to fly there to get the operators set up. Silver lining to all that hassle from the outages is that they want me there for the plant's official launch, which is a pretty big deal. This will be the biggest coal power plant of its kind. There will be a lot of international media coverage. They're going to fly me on the corporate jet, even," he said, proud of his big-time work and feeling on top of his game in his field.

"Dad, isn't the world trying to figure out how to use less fossil fuels to reverse the effects of global warming that they cause?" Kora mostly self-censored her words and tried not to get into it with her dad, but she was tired and suddenly felt like saying what she had been wanting to say for so long. It slipped out. The debate began.

"I know you're not thrilled with my business, Kora, but it's what fuels the world and what puts food in your stomach. One day you'll understand that the technology I design is the bleeding edge of innovation, state of the art, and that's why I'm crushing it with my patent on the newest industry-standard technology. You don't have to make money for a living yet, so you don't understand."

Kora retaliated: "Dad, this is only the beginning. Things are going to get worse if we don't start making decisions based on the health of the planet. Can't you get involved in solar or wind power instead with your tech skills? Those don't have as much impact on the atmosphere as coal. Isn't it already known that the fossil fuels being extracted from the earth and then burned are what's causing the global warming problem, affecting people all over the world?" When she started speaking from her heart, it came pouring out.

"Kora, my industry doesn't seem to be slowing down. You want to change the way energy is used in the world, but it will take decades to change the infrastructure. It's naive to think otherwise. Right now, I'm doing the best I can, helping coal power plants run cleaner. Give me some credit," her father said.

There was a stalemate.

Her father's eyes turned angry, and he went off: "I'm an engineer. I create technology that makes dirty power sources a little bit cleaner. The software taps into data from thousands of sensors placed around a coal plant to help operators make better decisions and to optimize coal plant function. This Russian one—I'm installing it. I've been hired and given big money because I'm an expert. Imagine how much black smoke would be coming from its smokestacks if I didn't help with this innovation."

Duncan had given the sales pitch millions of times to power plant officials all over the world. He knew how to convince the megacorporations they were in some way being "environmentally sensitive" by using his software. But saying it to Kora, he felt slightly like a sellout. He knew that she would see right through his claims of helping with carbon neutrality while still supporting and working with the fossil fuel industry. He was used to preaching to the choir. The clients thought he was brilliant, a hero who was helping them perpetuate an age-old business that had recently gotten pressure to change. Defending himself to his daughter made him feel vulnerable, like when he had tried to defend himself from her shaming and disappointed looks when he twisted the top off a single-use water bottle that would serve him for no more than twenty minutes and then sit in a landfill for another four generations.

"Dad, I think you and the work you are doing are part of the problem. The earth is falling apart all around us. When will you think it will finally be time to take action? How can it be OK for you to continue to work for the industry that is causing global warming, pulling fossil fuels out of the earth to be burned? What you are doing is causing the climate crisis. And I don't feel good about it."

There, she said it. She had never confronted her dad like this. Something woke up in her to speak her mind. And she spoke from the heart and dumped it all out on her dad. How could she handle disagreeing with her parent, her only parent, on matters she felt passionate about and he found laughable? Kora really felt like he was siding with evil, dancing with the enemy. She was disappointed and embarrassed by his position and his deplorable contributions to the world.

"I can't stop the people and governments and businesses that want to build this, but I can help them run cleaner," Duncan offered.

"But you're smart enough to help figure out a real solution—clean energy! How can you not believe climate change is real and intensifying, Dad? How can you not want to stop it? Your own wife was killed in a record-breaking wildfire. Climate change killed Mom, and we will suffer the rest of our lives from that. . . . You don't believe that change can be made? That it needs to be made? Will next summer have even bigger fires, even more catastrophic? Who else has to die to make this real to you?" Her voice quivered.

Bringing up Blythe and her death made Duncan freeze up. It was like a dagger into his heart, pushing the button that would leak all the unresolved emotions he had so nicely tucked away under his breastplate of armor since she died. He closed his eyes and fought back his tears. He was trained by his father that men don't cry, but he so wished he could right then.

"Kora, don't you ever blame me and my work for your mom's death," he snapped back. "That's not fair. It was a fluke accident, and I wish it didn't happen just as much as you do. That was out of our control." He fought a crack in his voice as he took an emotional hit to his gut that made him feel sick to his stomach. He told himself it was a ludicrous and illogical claim by his own teenage daughter, who was obviously confused, disturbed, and still dealing with PTSD from the tragedy of losing her mom.

Kora shook her head, her chest becoming tight and her breath shallow. "No, Dad, we could have done something. We can still do something to save someone else's wife or mother. We make choices every day. This is happening all over the world, one climate-related disaster event after another. Other people are losing their moms from hurricanes and floods and fires every day, not to mention cancers and lung diseases from pollution. Why won't you see? There's more carbon dioxide in our atmosphere than at any other time in human history, Dad. How much have you helped put there?"

Duncan rolled his eyes. "You really think that humans can some- how control nature? Do you think we have superpowers to make hur- ricanes and droughts and floods and wildfires stop happening? Since when do we have any say in the weather? If we could control weather, we would make it rain on crops, we would call upon the wind to blow away the bad air quality, ski resorts would order up snow, and I would make sure it was seventy-seven degrees with a slight tropical breeze during my one-week Hawaiian vacation each year. Humans wish they had that power. But we don't. Nature does what it wants, it's an act of God. That's why we invented air conditioners! My job has nothing to do with your outrageous nonsense."

He went on, and was not about to be interrupted.

"Don't you like the lights in your home? Having a refrigerator and fresh food? Getting driven around in your car? The internet, air- conditioning, TV, radio, Netflix? I tell you, you have a really good life, Kora, much better than you would have had in Ecuador, where people still hover around one kerosene lamp to do homework and cook over open fires. You want to go out and find your own wood to burn every day? Their life is hard. They wish they had some constant electricity so they could have an easier life as you do. I don't think they would care where their energy came from as long as it could keep their food cool or allow their water to be pumped from a well right into a faucet into their kitchen without having to walk and carry it every day. Everything we do takes energy, so don't make me feel like the bad guy. I am helping bring power to those who have been left behind."

Kora was shocked by the racism and elitism of her father's statements, but she had to speak up. "Dad, a government's scientists don't just put out a report on climate change for no reason. The findings have proved time and time again that it is us, human activity, causing all this climate destruction. Why are you looking the other way? Why are you dismissing the experts? We all need to start doing something about it, now. Otherwise, it's only going to get worse."

Duncan scoffed, too angry to be kind. "Science can be arbitrary. You can use it one way or the other to prove your point. Don't you know that data can be manipulated and analyzed in any way you want the outcome to be? You can't believe everything you read. You're just an alarmist, Kora, and you're buying into all the hype." Kora knew that there was no changing her dad. It was clear that she needed to create the change she wanted to see in the world, on her own, and possibly with the help of others who had seen the light. Her dad was a lost cause.

Two days later, Duncan spent twelve hours trying to get comfortable in the VIP jet's extra-large leather seat, with his eye mask on and his travel pillow around his neck, but he never got in that just-right position. He hated flying, because he was forced to stay still. He put his wireless headphones on, but his sadness barreled down on him, as a heavy feeling of aloneness ached within. Kora was the only family he had anymore, and their connection was far from close. They were at an impasse.

Before Kora's dad's carbon footprint touched down on Russian soil, through the tablet he left behind in their living room, Río popped up and told Kora of his exciting new plan for her to go foil the world's largest coal power plant before it could be ignited.

CHAPTER 27

FROM RUSSIA, WITH LOVE FOR THE EARTH

RURAL RUSSIA

Kora had a slight twinge when she thought of how the destruction of the coal plant would affect her father. Even though she knew that this would hurt him very personally, she also knew she had to act in the way that would benefit the most people and the earth. EcoQueen's path was clear: she needed to blast the coal plant with her powers before it could be fired up.

Río had hacked into Duncan's plans for the plant. His research confirmed that EcoQueen's electrical charge would cause significant damage if she could just touch the server that connected the plant's central nervous system. Her dad designed systems with backups, but her channeled powers could melt through all his built-in protections. Río and Kora had made a checklist of all the steps EcoQueen needed to take to evade security, destroy the power plant, and get back safely.

Everything went almost completely according to plan, except for the nail-biting delay on EcoQueen's extraction. She could practically feel the breath of the security guards as they rushed toward the control room. The video feed of her taking the coal plant off-line must have mesmerized Río enough to distract him from the important work-arounds he needed to do in order to get EcoQueen out through a monitor she had bricked with her superpowers. Precious seconds ticked away.

"Get me out of here, Río! Get me back, bro, they're coming!" Her desperate call snapped him back to the task at hand. But when he tried to upload the code they needed, it didn't work. He tried again—nothing.

"I know, I know. I'm working on it, EcoQueen," Río muttered to himself. The video feed blinked out. His internet was usually completely reliable because of the redundancy he'd built in; he knew that his sister's life might depend on reliable communications or on him getting her out of sticky situations. He didn't have any data to indicate why all the regular systems were down. He had disturbing flashbacks to the recent blackout when EcoQueen was in Congo. He hated losing all his data and all his control.

"Río, it's time for me to go!"

Río felt a flutter of panic at EcoQueen's whisper, but he processed the fact that at least he could still hear her. He took a calming breath, turned on a hot spot, and hit the keys again.

"Use that computer on the far left," Río directed.

EcoQueen pressed her palm to the monitor, blank but still hot from the surge she had caused. She zipped on her digital way back through her father's iPad in their hotel suite.

As her feet dangled off his desk, Kora felt the impact of what she had just done to the one person on earth who had cared for her the longest. Duncan wasn't the most emotionally or physically present of fathers, but he was the only dad she'd known, and she had destroyed his life's work with one touch of her hand.

Her father was probably tearing his hair out in a hotel room in Russia. He had been prepared for a day of glory, but now his career had crashed along with the systems of the coal plant. Instead of press conferences of ribbon cuttings and handshakes, his next few hours would hold disastrous data, embarrassing phone calls, and humiliating in-person meetings with the people who thought they had hired the world's foremost authority on systems software for power plants and now were sorely disappointed.

She remembered how disturbed her dad had been when the power went off at their house on her thirteenth birthday. His panic now would be unmanageable.

Kora realized that this was all her fault. She had put her father in a very difficult position. Her dad's reputation would be permanently tarnished. He might lose his job and not be able to pay the significant mortgage on the home they were trying to rebuild.

But Kora also realized that if she hadn't taken action to destroy the power plant, the earth would have continued its hurtling path to climate disasters at a far accelerated pace.

Because she had stood up for the environment and because the destruction of the coal plant was so substantial, the global power conglomerate was going to suffer huge losses. They wouldn't be able to pay for the extraction of more coal. This was a big opportunity for green energy companies that had been bidding against them around the world. Clean, green wind-, solar-, and hydropower plants were now clearly a much better investment. EcoQueen's action would change the economy and change the world, all for the better.

Kora would try to use her daughterly love to help her dad get through whatever challenges she'd caused him with her EcoQueen powers. She and her dad were both stronger than they thought. They'd been crushed by her mom's death, but maybe they could honor her memory and what was left of their family by working together to get through this. She could ask Bodi to help her look up some family therapist recommendations tomorrow.

As she tried to process all her emotions, a flash from behind her interrupted her thoughts. Río appeared on her dad's monitor. His forehead was covered with sweat, and his eyes looked panicked.

"I'm coding your teletransport to Australia. Everything is on fire. We need EcoQueen right now."

CHAPTER 28

REUNION

AUSTRALIA

Río had no choice but to bring EcoQueen right to the next mission. Australia was burning, and it was finally time that she journeyed there. As she traveled on the broadband, EcoQueen hung on for dear life, closing her eyes while time, space, and matter flew by her, and once again, she had no idea exactly where she was going to land.

Australia was suffering its hottest and driest year on record, void of rainfall. The vegetation had been cooked to perfect tinder fuel as sparks jumped and started new fires in forests that were literally standing matchsticks. The record heat and dryness created some of the most apocalyptic early season fire activity ever witnessed in the country. So far, fifteen million acres of Australia had burned. Firefighters fought the fires as if they were up against a wall of flames with squirt guns. No one could contain this wrath—it would just have to destroy everything in its path until there was nothing left to burn.

Already, thousands of people had evacuated to the beaches when the flames came dangerously close to their homes, saving nothing but their lives, and they were lucky enough to be evacuated by military ships and aircraft. But some were not as lucky, including the animals whose habitat was burning.

That week, Australia had its hottest day in recorded history, as daily highs across the nation hit an average of 105.6 degrees Fahrenheit. The very next day broke that record with temperatures at 107.4 degrees Fahrenheit. This day, EcoQueen's first time in Australia, happened to be the hottest temperature reliably measured on earth in any December. No different than cancer untreated, global warming out of control would keep getting worse.

Kora landed in a room where three people stared at her. It was hot and the fire was near. EcoQueen's mouth was dry, and her eyes felt like she had sandpaper under her eyelids impeding the mechanism of blinking properly. She couldn't take a deep breath as hot ash replaced fresh air. She felt a dim headache setting in, but the excitement and energy of being in this room, with these people, seemed to overpower the effects of the poor air quality, even as ash lightly dusted the ground like snow.

As each second ticked by, one more eucalyptus, filled with its flammable sap, ignited the next tree, which created the spark that jumped into the next canopy, and this repeated across the whole continent. A half billion wild animals like koalas and kangaroos ran with singed feet to evacuate their burning habitat, without a drink of water to be found. The fire traveled faster than most animals could ever run.

The three people stood, expecting her. They were not at all shocked by her clumsy entry into the light. This time, EcoQueen came rolling out of Río's desktop computer, in the room where he had spent years developing the technology through which she had transported. Mission control was meticulously clean and looked like an office at NASA where servers, cameras, scanners, and printers blinked. Three large computer monitors showed various sites and data representations: simultaneously pumping, churning, generating, and calculating about the next mission at hand, the one in Río's very own backyard in New South Wales.

Río had a poster of the periodic table framed on the wall, as well as a portrait of an unrecognizable celebrity, Sir Tim Berners-Lee from the UK, the man who invented the World Wide Web, the first web browser, and the fundamental protocols and algorithms allowing the web to scale. The poster of the nondescript middle-aged balding man in a blue blazer was framed, under glass, but the ashes of the fires had already begun creating a residue over it.

EcoQueen had become accustomed to getting herself oriented to her new location in just a few intentional breaths while her eyes scanned. She shook out her cape, patted down her body to shake off the ash, straightened herself up a bit and said, "Hi," giving a little wave. She whipped her cape behind her and tried to appear grounded, as if she'd gotten off the elevator on the wrong floor and quickly needed to adapt to the unfamiliar surroundings.

This was a first, to arrive at a mission greeted by people who were expecting her. For several seconds, everyone stood amazed and excited and stunned. EcoQueen was confused but sensed an inclusive feeling radiating from the three other people in the room.

As her mind slowly put it all together, she recognized Río, living and in the flesh, standing in the room of computers. A calm came over her that felt like this was precisely where she needed to be.

Río could not contain himself. He barreled up to EcoQueen and embraced her in a big real-life bear hug. His excitement bubbled out. "Finally you are here and we can meet you in person! We need your help! Right now!" Río blurted.

EcoQueen responded, "You know my superpowers, Río. I clearly don't have the power to put this fire out."

"Our cure is ready, and we need your help, not only to put the fires out here in Australia but to help restore balance for the whole world!" he said, not realizing that his introductory communication with EcoQueen lacked context and explanation. He stuttered and fought to spit out the words he had been waiting to tell Kora, his sister. His eyes focused up and into the corner of the ceiling, where the walls met, searching to find the language floating somewhere up there in space. When they talked through screens, he applied an anti-stutter algorithm that he designed to fix his broken speech, but in person, it was not as smooth. With a perma-grin that almost curved around his face from ear to ear, he managed to deliver what he wanted to say for so long.

"I am . . . I am . . . I-I-I . . . am Río. Your brother—*river* in Spanish."

The others in the room were looking at EcoQueen in awe. They had been awaiting her arrival in person for years, actually her whole lifetime. They knew her superpowers were needed in other parts of the world where global warming was spinning out of control. Other places were being ravaged and destroyed, other communities were fleeing, being evacuated, so they had been patient as she did her work, but now their home was the one in danger. And so she was finally called to join the team. They had been counting the moments until they could hug their baby in real life; over a decade and a half after she had been adopted, EcoQueen was finally in her biological family's home.

Without any words, the woman in the room, who had been reeling those first few moments and overtaken with emotion, finally got it together and stepped in front of EcoQueen. They were exactly the same height, with similar petite builds. The older woman burst out crying.

The forty-something-year-old mom cradled EcoQueen's soft face between her hands and looked into the eyes of this relative that she had never seen in person since she was a few days old. "My baby, my baby, I am so sorry!" Her first words to her biological daughter, her son's twin, the child she left back in Ecuador.

Avalon's hair was dirty blonde, with a swath of gray hair ribboned down from her left temple. Her face was full of freckles that blended together in groups of threes and fours, expressing just how much time she had spent outside under the sun. Avalon had the body of a person you could tell would get thinner as she aged. She wore a few necklaces, an impressive-looking stone pendant, and some colorful beads around her neck and wrists, as an attempt to garner some strength and power from the stones she chose.

EcoQueen almost lost her footing and nearly fell over as she processed the fact that her biological mom was standing right in front of her. The woman, the other mom who EcoQueen had wondered about almost daily and who she recognized from those strange visions, was embracing her in a hug that was nearly holding her up. Hugging her mom's body felt strange at first. Was this real? But the longer the hug went on, the more significant the feeling of coming home became. It was a strange sensation that she couldn't quite register intellectually. Mother and child melted into each other's embrace. Love was the only thing holding them up on their shaky legs.

Kora listened to her mom's breath, with each exhale a stuttering cry of air that had been held for the last seventeen years finally being released. For the first time, they both felt that feeling of well-being and security together, the feeling that one gets only from being enveloped in the protective embrace of one's own mom.

EcoQueen finally spoke, sharing a teary moment with the stranger who was close family.

"So . . ." She drew that conjunction out long enough to compose her reaction into words. "I lost my birth mom, but found an adopted mom. Then I lost my adopted mom to climate change, and then found my birth mom because of climate change? Is that what is going on here?" Kora asked aloud.

"I can't believe I am finally meeting you. I have not been able to feel complete since I lost you," Avalon said through her overwhelming emotion. Her eyes welled up with tears.

As the snowball of love kept gaining momentum, Kora looked over to the last stranger in the room. She would have assumed that if this was her mom and that was her brother, he must be her father. From her visions of the young man in the Amazon and his physical resemblance to her, she was sure that this was her biological dad.

Joaquin was older now; his long black hair was the same shade, length, and thickness as EcoQueen's, but with a few strands of gray marking time lived. His shaman energy made him larger than life to her. As soon as Joaquin stepped in front of EcoQueen, she saw into her own soul. All her ancestors flashed from seven generations back up until the present moment of her finally standing in line with this man, her biological father. His green eyes looked as if they were painted from the same circle in the watercolor set as hers, and the tone of their skin was identical in the shade as well, torn from the same cloth. She instantly felt connected. His essence was so familiar.

His face was wrinkled but wise and revealed his purpose on earth. His life energy had been poured into climate justice work. He was an Amazonian Waorani living in Australia, studying with the Aboriginal peoples on the continent, still seeking ways to keep the balance on earth.

He had spent several years on the run in Ecuador, single-handedly trying to undo all the fossil fuel operations that were going on in his beloved Amazon. As they dug, he buried; as they built, he unbuilt; as they brought in heavy machinery, he disabled the machinery, foiling oil development and explorations with a secret team who also believed in the importance of protecting the earth over profits. Their goal was to protect the natural world above anything else. Joaquin was one of the most wanted men in Ecuador, not for selling drugs, nor violence, nor trafficking, but for the setbacks he created for the fossil fuel industry. He disrupted business as usual in the name of Mother Earth, and this was considered criminal by some. His people thought the contrary . . . that to deface Mother Earth was behavior deserving punishment.

Joaquin still was the keeper of the last sacred seed, upholding the commitment to his land and his people. The one sacred seed remained in his careful possession. He had kept it close to him, safe and protected, until he was reunited with Avalon, who had never stopped searching for him. Together they had been working on something monumental that was about to come to fruition, after many years of research and development and nurturing of the power of the sacred seed. They believed that they had developed the cure for Mother Earth and the global warming disaster that was affecting all living beings around the world.

Joaquin's hands were thick and leathery from interacting with soil most of his life and from using them as his main tools in his work. He reached out and held each of EcoQueen's more delicate hands, and rubbed them with his thumbs. Joaquin was almost unable to believe he was finally holding the hands of his daughter, lost to their family before he had even had a chance to meet her. They both became lost in a different universe together now, downloading their ancestry right there in the pools of each other's irises.

"We have been watching your accomplishments and your earth-saving actions, your heroic saves, and your service to the planet as Río has been assisting you on these missions. We are so proud of you. You have been chosen for a challenging job. But you have been doing it so well," Joaquin said.

Kora let those words, delivered with such love and pride by her biological dad, land in her heart and mind for one glorious, long moment. It felt so good to be praised, as she had not been given any credit for her heroic actions until that moment. It got old being an unsung superhero. It was lonely crossing the globe on her own, trying to put out the devastating effects of global warming as a one-woman show.

"Thank you. But I don't know if I am making a difference any-more. It's almost impossible to stop the destructive weather events, hurricanes, fires, droughts, floods, heat waves, and everything danger-ous that the rising temperatures are bringing. It feels like this work is never-ending. I have tried, but I think this problem is way bigger than what one girl out there trying to use superpowers against climate change can do. It is too big and raging out of control."

"No, *mija*, every little bit helps. Each action that someone does can be productive, we need to keep that up! Everyone needs to do their part, and do whatever they can. And this is what you can do. You and Río can reach out and inspire them. Do not let yourself lose hope! We may have reached the point where catastrophic events are happening at an unprecedented rate and we are at a tipping point, but we have a plan, a possible cure. That is why we finally called you back to us. We wanted to earlier, but you were doing such important work, we couldn't pull you away. The earth needs you and your powers now more than ever. We may have what it takes, but we have to tackle it together."

Avalon jumped in. "We understand the dangers. Swift action has not been taken by leaders and governments to turn this thing around, so we are ready to take matters into our own hands and do something now! Our planet's home is on fire, and we need to react like the emer-gency it is. We cannot wait any longer."

Joaquin added, "A Cree prophecy states that when the earth is rav-aged and the animals are dying, a tribe of people from all races, creeds, and colors will put their faith in deeds and not words to make the earth green again." He paused a moment to let this sink in with everyone in the room. And then he continued, "Humanity is failing to protect the air, the water, and the land as a priority over progress. But we have a way to reintroduce the balance, something that we believe will turn this climate crisis around." He grew animated, excited to finally have the whole family together for the big reveal.

Kora looked squarely in her birth father's eyes and nodded her head. "Count me in. Let's do it!" EcoQueen was ready to take action. She added, "Doing something is way better than doing nothing. I guess we are all here together at this time in history in order to step it up to the next level and to help start a new cycle of sustainability."

Joaquin gathered the family members in the room into a huddle. Heat from the drought conditions feeding the fire raging nearby was making them all sweat, but he encircled his arms around Avalon, Río, and EcoQueen with the wingspan of an eagle and brought them in.

"We have everything to lose if we don't act right now! We are in the danger zone, and there is a threat to people's lives, safety, homes, and habitat. If we don't address it now, we are failing to protect Aweidi, Mother Earth, the place we all call home, our children—the next generation. Until governments and people in power can dramatically curtail greenhouse gas emissions and work to turn global warming around, we need to do it ourselves. And here is the plan. We have been working on this for years, and we are finally ready to execute."

He pulled out the leather satchel that was tucked under his white linen shirt, which had hung around his neck by a thin leather cord since he was a teenager. It was the same one he had been protecting since being given the responsibility from the shaman back in the Ecuadorian rainforest that he was now a refugee from.

Avalon chimed in, "We have been working on what we believe can reverse the effects of global warming! Now is the time the elders take the hands of the children and guide them to take action. We think we have figured out an innovative master plan that may finally get us out of this climate crisis. I was able to clone and propagate the sacred seed that your dad was entrusted with. It embodies the powers you have, plus the accelerated powers of reforestation, regeneration, carbon sequestration—plus a little magic wrapped up in it. We believe that if they are planted in the most vulnerable ecosystems, the places hit hardest by climate change, these sacred seeds can potentially regenerate all that has been destroyed due to climate change."

Avalon carefully touched the leather satchel, which now held five seeds. Her life's work had come to fruition. She felt proud and excited, confident her science would work. She was so ready to implement it, now that she had her special team together.

Río, who had helped in the gene cloning of the magical seed, explained what he and his mom had done.

"We used ancient techniques of cloning seeds combined with cutting-edge bioengineering. We took the one remaining seed that Dad had from the rainforest and shaved off a tiny piece of it carefully without damaging the embryo. We ground that bit into a powder that Mom analyzed with genome-mapping technology. She did not genetically modify it, she just learned how to sequence and clone the special seed. We think we have it."

Joaquin added, "These seeds are small but rich with possibilities: when these sacred seeds are planted, they have the potential to save the world. This is what we need to do now, since nothing else is working. Planting these seeds at the same time will combine the potential energy for global restoration and achieve decarbonization. These seeds are the medicine. Our future is in your hands."

In the huddle, Río gave out directions. He had been planning and replanning this moment for many months, over and over in his head, combing through all details, strategies, flowcharts, and spreadsheets. He had it mapped out in a way that had been swirling around in his mind, and the challenge would be how to get it out of his head and communicated to his family clearly. Once he could lock into the action plan, his stutter disappeared and he delivered.

"I have set coordinate points on the teletransporters for each of you. Dad will take this seed back to the Amazonian rainforest, the zone of the greatest deforestation on earth. One and a half acres of rainforest are lost every second, that's one and a half soccer fields . . . a second!" Río caught himself going off on research and data and knew he needed to pull himself back to the mission at hand.

Joaquin interjected to help get Río back on track. Over the years, he had learned how to help his son utilize his special spectrum mind to its highest level. "Prompt reforestation would solve a significant percentage of the global warming problem, and the new growth forests would automatically begin to help suck carbon from the atmosphere. Your mother and I have seen the sacred seed work there before. But now we have five seeds!"

Joaquin held the familiar red seed in his aging hand, and flashbacks rushed in from the time he dropped the sacred seed, before he had to leave their mother, before he knew he was going to be a father. He felt the potential of the little teardrop seed vibrating in his hand, ready to get to work.

The original seed was passed on by his people to be planted when the end of the world—of species and biodiversity, and the health of the earth—was at stake. It was bad when he first decided to use the seed, but it was even worse now. He was absolutely confident that this was the right time to plant again.

"We must harness our power collectively and come together in a much larger way with a singular focus to heal. This is the only way we are going to evolve as a society and put an end to all this madness! This is the balancing force for nature."

Río blurted out again, "Mum predicts that these seeds will allow the earth to recover from the damage that has been done to it since the industrial revolution and will cause a massive *shift* for humanity in the most positive direction possible on a level that has not yet been reached on planet Earth!!" He repeated from memory the exact words Avalon had once told him.

Río continued with his data as a cue for the next stage of the plan. "Arctic sea ice has melted down to about 1.32 million square miles. All the sea level–rise threats originate from the shrinking of the Arctic ice and the melting of the permafrost. The melt has a direct effect on the extreme weather events we are dealing with. The Arctic is currently warming twice as fast as the rest of the world. So, Mum will go and plant this seed there."

"Yes, Río, we hope that this seed helps to recalibrate the temperatures there and puts the Arctic back into the deep freeze we need, stabilizing the permafrost and glaciers. Once the seed creates the balance again, the moss, algae and lichen, and cyanobacteria growth will revive. And it will also rejuvenate the depleted seaweeds and deep-sea kelp, all so crucial but failing right now." Avalon gently placed her seed in a satchel similar to Joaquin's and put it around her neck for safekeeping. She held the pouch tenderly with both hands in prayer pose, putting a little wish and hope into it, as desperate times take desperate measures. She had put all of her life's energy into being able to perpetuate these sacred seeds so they could do their rehabilitating work, and now she was eager to see if her science would work magic.

This was all happening so quickly. EcoQueen had just been reintroduced to her family, her people, and they were all about to scatter. Yet, they were helping her in her mission, so she knew they were all in it for the same reason. To heal the planet.

Her birth family had some of the same kinds of gifts and powers—and the same desire—to heal the earth as she was born with. She felt a greater sense of confidence that, together, they probably had a better chance of making significant change than she did going it alone. She felt proud to be part of this powerhouse of a family. Working together, she was sure they would be a force of nature. She was so impressed by her family's passion, their brains, and their action. She was so proud to be a part of this effort and trusted them completely.

Río finished the game plan. "My sister, EcoQueen, will go to the Great Barrier Reef. Lucky for you, that is close by. Half of this coral reef is already dead and bleached from rising ocean temperatures and acidity in the water. Actually, 81 percent of reefs have been bleached and have died off already in the northern sector of the Great Barrier Reef, and this is happening to coral all around the planet as seawater warms. Hopefully, the sacred seed will help the dying reef renew through the growth of healthy seaweeds, seagrasses, sea lettuce, and an important algae called crustose coralline algae that forms a symbiotic relationship with coral. And we intend for it to replenish the mangrove plants. Although they do not live underneath the surface of the water completely, mangrove plants grow along the shores near the Great Barrier Reef and help stabilize the shoreline. Their roots filter the waters around the coral reefs by removing the pollutants." Río paused, now that he had delivered another heavy plate of information.

Joaquin gently passed one more sacred seed to EcoQueen in a protective leather satchel. While holding both of her hands firmly in his tight grip, her biological father instructed her, "Bring this seed to the coral reef, and drop it there, where we may have a chance of restoring it back to health. We cannot lose that ecosystem."

"I'm on it! This is my jam!" EcoQueen said, so glad to be doing this as a team effort after circling the globe doing this kind of work alone. It felt so much better to be working together to make great changes. She believed in herself, and in her family.

Río finished up the directions: "After you get to your assigned destinations through my teletransport program, we will know when the moment is to plant the seed. Trust me. Trust yourself. Trust what we are doing. This can only work if the seeds are dropped at the location at the same time. Synchronized, the seeds' power can jolt the earth in a way that puts it back into balance."

EcoQueen said, "That is three seeds, and three locations, but what about you, Río? I thought we had four new seeds ready, plus the original to hold in reserve. What if Río launched a seed into the sky? Could it penetrate the layer in the atmosphere that is causing the greenhouse effect and help the air quality, too?"

Joaquin smiled. "Yes, Avalon and I had been considering that. You think like us!" This made EcoQueen smile deeply, feeling solidarity. "That will be the fourth seed. The fifth seed, the original entrusted to me, we will guard for future generations."

Joaquin turned and looked into the same green eyes as his, but in the face of his son, and told him to do what he was told when he was around the same age. "We select you, Río, as the next keeper of the seeds. Do what you know to be right. The fight for Mother Earth is the mother of all fights."

EcoQueen helped with her agile fingers to put the last seed into a satchel and place it around Río's neck. She gave him a big hug and said, "Thank you, Río." EcoQueen kissed him on the forehead and felt a deep bond with these people, her family.

Río was pumped to be orchestrating the whole family. The responsibility of keeper of the seeds buoyed him instead of weighing him down. He said, "I have run the simulators so many times. The seeds are positive. Mum, Dad, EcoQueen: let's do this."

He put his headphones on, sat in his swivel chair in front of his four desktop screens, and put his hand on the mouse.

"OK? Everyone ready? Río, send us off!" Avalon exclaimed.

"I was born ready!" EcoQueen replied with delight.

The newly reunited family held hands before being separated again to all corners of the earth for the big job that needed to be done. They all embraced in a tight family hug until they felt the forces pulling them through the screen, through the fiber optics, the broadband, the satellite waves. The family flew through space and time, to use their combined superpowers to once and for all reverse the effects of global warming on their sacred planet Earth.

EcoQueen splashed out into the warmer-than-bath waters of the Great Barrier Reef. What once was covered in almost neon colors was now void of brightness and whitewashed. It was pale and sickly with few fish around chomping on the coral, because it was almost all dead.

Avalon popped out on the tundra in the Arctic, onto mushy exposed tundra soil that should have been buried under a sheet of ice.

Joaquin was ecstatic to be back in the misty and moist rainforest of his childhood, walking lightly on the scorched, deforested, desert-like depleted soil. He knew he could help regrow the rainforest. He had done it before. He still knew his way around. And he was confident in the power of the sacred seed.

Río fell deep into his programming trance, hacking what he felt was the purpose of the last of the cloned seeds. He preloaded his seed into the power air blaster he made that would propel it up into the atmosphere, past the smoke, into the sky above it all.

Finally, Río designed an image on his screen, an earth with a spiral around it. He infused it with the energy from the fifth seed. Without articulating what he'd programmed, he knew that the last frontier was to plant a seed in the minds of his generation. A seed to inspire people to protect, preserve, and take action.

Río created a prompt that would come up on every connected device in use in the world. The message said, "You are the last generation who can do something about climate change!" When each person put their finger on their device, with the picture of earth locked onto the screen, they would each get a little magic from the seed. That magic would inspire them to take action, now. It was much like the wake-up message after the global power outage, but superpowered to actually spur people to act.

The message and ensuing actions spread through the channels of social media and the internet. It seeded the data in the global information cloud. It penetrated everyone's consciousness in order to make the necessary shift to a healthy planet. Each individual began to create the change that was needed to turn this crisis around by being connected to each other and the natural resources of the places where they lived, all over the globe.

EcoQueen and her family planted their respective seeds at their four locations at the very same moment. The earth, to its core, felt the magic and power of the sacred seeds taking root in the most impacted and vulnerable ecosystems. The spinning earth felt it, and the power resonated in all who inhabited it, everywhere. It was the shift, the change, the action that needed to happen to get us off the destructive trajectory into one of regrowth and rebuilding. It was a restart, and it enabled EcoQueen and her family, together with people all over the world, to fend off the catastrophic effects of global warming for the planet, at least for now.

EPILOGUE

The sacred seeds did their job. They reversed the damage, destruction, and pollution that humans had caused in the last two hundred years. But EcoQueen's family's work was not over.

Joaquin took on the global project of helping plant new trees. He started an international organization called Seas of Trees that planted trees for every occasion, thousands of them at a time, anywhere he could find dirt to plant them. Río would sell his patented algorithm for teletransportation to technology companies for billions of dollars, eliminating the need for cars and airplanes, which allowed people to travel without using fossil fuels anymore. He dumped that money into Avalon's latest scientific research projects. She built labs to help plant species on the verge of extinction to propagate.

Duncan did shift industries when he finally understood that a whole infrastructure change needed to occur. He invested his money and his intellect into the emerging market of tidal energy, creating electricity from the natural rising and falling of the tides. Kora was very proud of him, and he was proud of Kora. He never did find out that she was behind the power plant failure in Russia, though.

Kora went on to study climate science in California, although she would often teletransport to visit with her biological family in Australia. Now that everything had settled with the climate, she would go for dinner and discussion instead of epic adventures.

Bodi became Kora's boyfriend, and they surfed and biked a lot between their studies, which were focused on desalinization to make fresh water for the world.

AUTHOR'S NOTE

At the completion of this book, in November 2020, the global average atmospheric carbon dioxide rate is 409.8 parts per million (ppm for short), the highest level at least in the last eight hundred thousand years. This is why students have been protesting for their future and the health of the planet. The global CO_2 emissions are about 37 billion metric tons per year, and we're on track to raise temperatures by 3 degrees Celsius by 2100. To have a shot at maintaining a climate suitable for humans, the world's nations most likely have to reduce CO_2 emissions drastically from the current level—to perhaps fifteen billion or twenty billion metric tons per year by 2030. Then, through some kind of unprecedented political and industrial effort, we need to bring carbon emissions to zero by around 2050.

The best way to help tackle climate change is to use less fossil fuels personally in your daily life.

Drive less, fly in airplanes less, carpool more, ride your bike more, and walk.

Buy less junky stuff, shop locally, and be aware of how far your product has traveled.

Make your home more efficient. Turn down the heat. Manage your refrigerants. Make sure your appliances are energy efficient, and dispose of old appliances responsibly, to be recycled properly.

Choose renewable energy produced from solar and wind power when you can.

Buy organic foods, locally grown and in season when possible. Compost your food waste to change it back into soil. Reduce food waste and try to eat a plant-rich diet.

Bring your own reusable bags and cups and avoid single-use plastics.

Plant a tree! Support reforestation projects, help conserve tropical rainforests and forests close to you. Check out www.seasoftrees.org, who will plant trees for you.

Stay educated and help other children around the world to stay in school, especially girls.

***

Upon completion of this book, choose one of these actions, and start doing it. Commit to one action you can do before closing this book.

The year that I finished writing this novel, which was over six years in the making, the weather devastation around the world got "biblical." I wanted to get this out sooner rather than later in order to help make students aware of the climate change predicament, educate on what is happening historically and scientifically, and empower you to get involved in the momentum and in conserving within your own lifestyle.

I wish the climate crisis could be fixed by one superhero, but really, you are the superhero. You have to take this into your own hands in order to change the way things work in the world. You have the ability to make this planet, your home, better than it was left to you. Please be active in this cause.

You are the first generation to understand this problem of climate change entirely, and maybe one of the last to be able to do anything about it. Have hope. You can make change.

ACKNOWLEDGMENTS

Thank you to all who have picked up this book and read it to the end. I hope it inspired you to take action and stand up for our beautiful earth we call home.

Thank you to Shoshana Brower, my mother-in-law, who had the original idea to dress up as EcoQueen for Halloween with her grandkids. That gave me inspiration to dream up a superhero who had the powers to reverse global warming.

Thank you to my husband, Daniel, who believed in me the whole time and helped me to get over the finish line and complete this book that you hold in your hand and read.

Thank you to Emily Shoff, my writing coach, who helped me get the story out of my head and onto the page.

Thank you, Tegan Tegani, for being a brilliant editor.

Thank you, Gerald Measer, my dad, who has always been my greatest fan and gets behind any endeavor I set out to achieve in my life.

ABOUT THE AUTHOR

Joanna Measer Kanow has been an environmentalist her whole life, which led her to get a Conservation and Resource Studies degree at UC Berkeley. She has worked in green building, on alternative-energy projects, as an environmental educator and activist, and as a carbon-neutral facilitator. She is also a life coach and author.

Joanna has always aimed to encourage people to care for the environment, fostering their development as stewards of the earth's natural balance. She now runs a tree-planting nonprofit organization called Seas of Trees, which she founded to help combat climate change. Proceeds from this book will help fund this organization's mission to take climate action now by planting trees and encouraging youth to get involved in environmental stewardship.

Joanna resides in Telluride, Colorado, with her two daughters and husband, where she spends most of her free time deep in nature, hiking, biking, and skiing. *EcoQueen* is her debut novel.

CPSIA information can be obtained
at www.ICGtesting.com
Printed in the USA
FSHW010353270321
79897FS